Here's Lower

Lennie Lower, Sydney 1930.

Here's Lower

Lennie Lower

Illustrated by Patrick Cook

Compiled by Tom Thompson

ETT IMPRINT
Exile Bay

Published by ETT Imprint, Exile Bay in 2020

First published by Hale & Iremonger 1983
Illustrations © Patrick Cook 1983
Selection and Introduction © Tom Thompson 1983, 2020

ETT IMPRINT
PO Box R1906
Royal Exchange NSW 1225
Australia

ISBN 978-1-922473-09-7 (pbk)
ISBN 978-1-922473-10-3 (ebk)

The editor would like to thank Australian Consolidated Press and Cyril Pearl for permission to publish these columns.

Cover photograph by William Pidgeon, 1938, colourised.
Cover and internal design by Tom Thompson.

Contents

Lennie Lower: A Memoir
Cyril Pearl

Lennie Lower was held in enormous affection by the citizens of Sydney. With his friend and illustrator, W. E. Pidgeon ('Wep'), as distinguished an artist as Lower was a writer, he had become an integral part of Sydney life. In clubs and pubs, in lolly-shops and lunaparks, in the towering clinker-brick *château* of the millionaire pork-packer and the underground tiled *chalet-de-necessité* of the troubled pedestrian, in the streets and on the beaches, he was a man of infinite legend, a man of infinite laughs, a much-loved man. Even the Sydney taxi-driver, hunched ape-like over his frayed cigarette, would emit an approving, almost-human grunt if you asked him to deposit you at the newspaper office where Lower worked.

Lower's transcendent popularity is easily explained. He was an individualist in an era of creeping conformity. He was a rebel in a country of suffocating acquiescence. A Darlinghurst Don Quixote, he tilted at windbags, punctured pomposity, slaughtered sacred cows, all with tremendous gusto. He saw that much of life was absurd, and his laughter echoed down its stuffy corridors, lusty, irreverent and irrepressible.

As a humorist, Lower deployed a vast array of talents. He had a superb ear for dialogue, a searching eye for detail, a glorious sense of the ridiculous. He was a master of comedy in its multiform guises: subtle, vulgar, zany, verbal, ratbag, slapstick, nonsensical. His humour can be as realistic as a greasy sink, or as remote as the laugh of a leprechaun. He blends Tyl Eulenspiegel, Puck, Lewis Carroll, Edward Lear, W.S. Gilbert, P.G. Wodehouse, Groucho Marx and Roy ('Mo') Rene with a refreshing flavour of gumleaves.

When Lennie Lower died in 1947, I, as editor of the *Sunday Telegraph,* had the honour of devoting the leader-page to Lower's memory. I reprinted one of his delightful fairy-tales, and invited Wep to write a personal note about his old colleague.

This is what he wrote:

ONCE UPON A TIME THERE WAS
A FUNNY MAN ...

'There was once an aged bootmaker named Franz, who lived in a valley just crawling with mad bears.'

In the *Telegraph* ten years ago lots of whimsies began like that.

Now that their like can never appear again, we shall have to tell our own, and the prefix will be 'there was once Lennie Lower ...'

And, as long as his contemporaries' memories last, Lower will become part of the fable and legend he liked so much to build.

Even during his lifetime apocryphal stories about him were legion.

The average accepted image of the man was composed of hearsay evidence and an interpretation of him from his work.

It is a conglomerate picture of errant elf, harassed

householder, screwball and comic, that is likely to survive the reality.

The reality, indeed, was hard to find.

Close personal contact with him was difficult – he was too reserved and fundamentally shy to let anyone in behind the protective barriers of his personality.

There was much of the child in his makeup – he had its simplicity, irresponsibility, and, perhaps, its improvidence – certainly he had its fresh and devastating powers of observation.

He was one of those original spirits whose vision never wearies and who, in the common, unlooked-at aspects of life, finds always a new and amazing something.

How unerringly he cut those cameos of the standard husband-wife relationship – how much of everyone's domesticity was packed in so little.

And those wonderful journeys he took us into the lands of fairies and witches and giants and ogres!

It was his extraordinary keenness of observation and uncanny ability to assimilate the essence of a place or situation that gave salt and earthiness to his humour.

I remember long ago when I was with him on a caravan trip by the Snowy River being continually amazed at the apparently casual and indifferent attitude he adopted.

Yet not once did he fail to spot the local colour or pick the choicest cut of character.

I have never seen him scratch for, or alter a word. He caught the type with a dialogue of precision and economy that has scarce been matched since. Henry Lawson, too, did his piece for the man in the street.

He seemed to have few close friends, those nearest him were older but possessed of the same irresponsible adolescence.

It is hard to realize that he is dead.

For me and a million others he still lives while we can read.

His obituary is written, not in the newspapers, but in the trams, and the bars, and in the hearts of human men.

An Introduction

Tom Thompson

Officially, Lennie Lower didn't exist. When he was born in Dubbo on 3 September 1903, his father was on a bender and forgot to register the birth. From then on it was inevitable; Lennie's great obsessions with baby care, drunken husbands, flora, fruit and fauna were officially formed.

When Lennie was seven years old, his father died, his mother remarried and the family moved to Sydney. He joined the Royal Australian Navy after leaving school but found it too serious, and is believed to have deserted. As an 'ex-matelot' in the twenties, he often slept on trains or in Sydney's Domain, where he began recording tales.

His first published piece was in *Beckett's Budget,* a sleazy scandal sheet of 1926. In the following years he put daily comment under the name of T. I. Red in *The Labor Daily,* comment written 'with a dash of muriatic acid in his inkwell' as the harsh effects of the Depression hit NSW homes.

Here's Luck, his only novel, was published in 1930 and Lower quickly became Australia's most quoted humorist, writing up to eight columns a week for such papers as *The Daily Guardian, The Daily Telegraph, Smith's Weekly, The Sunday Telegraph* and *The Women's*

Weekly. With such a workload, he found that odd news items would often spark vivid and absurd imaginative writing.

This 'slapstick surrealism' wasn't dashed off instantaneously, for Lower would sit immobile at his desk, forehead on his typewriter, both arms dangling till he had set the joke in progress. He would then 'do an arabic' on the typewriter in his haste to get it all down pat.

Lennie Lower and tall stories go hand in hand. Copyboys allegedly had to drag him into work, still in his pyjamas. His office colleagues later confided:

> One day we heard ear splitting screams and cries for help from the room where Lower was working on his piece, perilously close to deadline as usual. 'Help, help!' shouted Lennie and several women rushed to the door. Lennie looked up from his typewriter and said mildly, 'Give me a cigarette, someone please.'

Lower loved drinking, but then Lower loved everything. His delight with the problems affecting fruit and vegetables, the comfort of wild and domestic animals, and the idiosyncrasies of the English language, were the main preoccupations in his later writing. Among the subjects that incurred his peculiar wrath and cynicism were 'The Government', and the 'Woman-as-Wife'. In letters to his own wife, Phyllis, he was always affectionate. Without 'Fleas', as Lower dubbed her, ordinary life became high drama:

> I have not got around to making the bed and I have called off the milkman who insisted on leaving hundreds of bottles of milk all over the outskirts of our occupied territory ... the insurance bloke called and demanded twelve bob which I reluctantly handed over ... After a

long search I failed to find the caretaker but found his rather buxom daughter in flat 16 and she informed that the rent was paid. I cheered loudly ...

That black tom cat calls on me each morning via the bedroom window and scares hell out of me every time ... I have not been watering your potplants because God has been doing that which I think is very sporting of him ... I went to a cafe in King Street and had some steak and tomatoes today. Four and ninepence. Wouldn't it!

For all his humour, in private Lower was a melancholic man. A colleague, Andrew Macdonald wrote:

Another outcome of Lower's dark introspections was the vital ingredient of all satiric comedy — the intense awareness that human beings, are, in themselves, so ludicrous that it is impossible to treat them seriously.

He was sacked by *The Telegraph* in 1940, over an historic meeting with Noel Coward. Whether he actually gave Mr Coward a 'king hit' is open to doubt, but certainly he found another job, back at *Smith's Weekly.* He joined the army and voiced his constant complaints in *Smith's Weekly, and Lennie Lower's Annual.*

When Lower died in Sydney Hospital on 10 July 1947, the obituaries for Australia's leading funny-man were slight. Cyril Pearl has suggested why:

It was of course a foolish day on which to die, even for a man with an exquisite sense of humour, because that day the linotypes were running hot with the news of the engagement of Princess Elizabeth and Lieutenant Phillip Mountbatten.

So it reached the gossip columns in *The Daily Telegraph* and *The Sydney Morning Herald;* the *Bulletin* gave him 19 lines. Only *Smith's Weekly* attempted to assess the man:

The great secret of Lower's humour is that he was always himself, he never let anyone or anything get in the way of his natural genius. Editors could tell him what to write about, he would go away and come back with something entirely different. Lennie Lower's humour was the real thing. It grew naturally as fruit and right out of life.

Lennie Lower, "working" at Jindabyne, 1940.

Be Kind to Landlords

*Kindness to Landlords Week has been officially
opened by an unemployed resident of Vaucluse,
who, taking advantage of the recent State legislation
in regard to rents, has invited his landlord to come
and live with him, providing he pays for his board.*

This kindly action might well be emulated and even
surpassed by those possessed of a kindly heart and the
will to do. Especially the will to do.

Landlords are a peculiar race. They are mostly visible
once a week, and then only at the front door. They ring
the door-bell carefully (being their own bell), or furiously,
for the same reason; or futilely, for the simple reason that
the tenant has crept into the ice-chest and pulled the door
shut, thus proving conclusively that he is out.

An outcast race, they live entirely on eviction notices,
which they gnaw in their garrets with great relish,
surrounded by bailiffs clamouring for their fees, which is
a quaint form of amusement.

It was only about five months ago that we, ourself,
became short of money. Most disturbing experience.
You've no idea. We had christened a pound note.
Smashed it in the face with a bottle of Pilsener and
declared the pound officially opened.

Landlord came grovelling for the rent on Monday.
Kicked him in the forehead as usual. Left at 2.30 in the

morning so as to save the neighbours any disturbance; took away all the lead off the roof, and in the bathroom, as a memento of our stay, and left a note signed anonymously by us, using another name on account of modesty.

We frequently meet him in the dole queue, but he bears no malice.

He is too weak.

Simple Talk on Dress

There is nothing more soul-shattering than to discover that you are wearing two left boots.

We are moved to mention this because Miss Dorothy Brunton in yesterday's paper said that 'One's clothes shape one's mental outlook.' Which is true. Look at the difference in mental outlook when a man wears his collar back to front!

Then again, notice when you're pulling your singlet off. For a moment you've got no outlook at all.

Mind you, it's not only the clothes. There's the manner of putting them on – carelessly or otherwise.

A man who puts his arm through one armhole of his vest and his leg through the other, ties the sleeves of his coat around his waist, and wears his hat round his neck for an amulet, shows a certain amount of carelessness in his dress which would be noticeable in very fashionable company.

Then there is the little matter of the socks matching the tie. This problem may easily be overcome. When buying socks, mention that you have a one- legged friend who would like a sock of the same pattern.

You may then wear two of the socks as socks, and the remaining one as a tie. After the feetsocks have been used for some months, they may be used as mittens. A good idea is to wear leggings, when you don't need any socks at all.

It beats us why clothing manufacturers have not made a shirt which has buttons down the back as well as in front. You could then wear it back to front when the exposed portion got a bit mouldy.

Ours not to reason why. We merely remain convinced that, had our mental outlook been properly clothed earlier, had we, instead of being attired in two pieces of soft rag and a safety pin, been clothed in a fireman's helmet at birth, with seaboots, a military overcoat, and motoring gloves, and eaten our porridge with a boat-hook, we should not have had to roll our own cigarettes this day.

MORAL: If you wear your trousers back to front, you have to kneel down to sit up. (Very deep.)

What Bread Is and How to Use It

About bread.
Bread is a large number of small holes entirely surrounded by bread.

A simple recipe for using it is to lay down a slice and put butter on top of same. This makes a palatable dish if you have the butter.

The price of flour – one of the ingredients of bread – has gone down. The price of bread has not gone down. There is, of course, a reason. We can't see it. But —

Bread-cart horses are eating more now than they did. Yeast has shown a decided tendency to rise, and the Viennese tradesmen engaged in making the swipes on top of Vienna loaves are demanding more money.

Cottage loaves have shown a decided falling off, on account of the operatives moving out of their cottages into flats.

On the whole, the situation is such that everyone should burst into tears and tell their friends that the country is going to the dogs.

Speaking of recipes, a good one for damper is:— Take 1 lb. flour, ½ lb. baking powder, 3 eggs, 1 grated prawn, and sufficient scones for nine people.

Eat scones. Stir remainder well.
Keep stirring. These are stirring times.

What Gold Is

How to Get It and Where It Is

It's not a bit of use looking for gold if you don't know where it is.

People are pegging out claims all over the place when they would be better employed pegging out the washing.

Gold is a metallic auriferous gold metal which is found in large or small single lumps, or linked together as is in gold watch-chains, or invisible, such as sovereigns.

Amateur prospectors must remember, however, that it is illegal to peg out a claim on a man's stomach just because he has a gold watch-chain.

Alluvial gold is found in creek-beds, waterholes, drain-pipes, and various other places. It is found on mountains and in valleys, etcetera.

It is also not found in many of the above places. That is the catch.

The best way to tell gold is to pass the nugget around a crowded bar, and ask them if it's gold.

If it comes back, it's not gold.

Strange Market Variations

It is about time the attention of the general public was drawn to the remarkable goings on in the vegetable and fruit markets. We gather from market reports that beans are very irregular. Questioned about this, the beans refused to give any information.

Bananas weakened, probably through neglect. Indeed, the report actually declares that buyers DID neglect the bananas, and consequently they weakened.

As for the market building itself, something should be done immediately, as it seems to be dangerous to human life. The day before yesterday the market was bolstered up. Shortly after this it fell. Then the bottom fell out of it. We understand that it is now rising again.

Take the peculiar conduct of green peas. They were very unsteady yesterday. They fell, rose again, became depressed, and then hardened. Later on, they seemed to be practically dead.

Potatoes, on the other hand, opened strongly, moved steadily, and were extremely strong towards the close of the day.

Watermelons were very brisk. We must visit the markets one of these days, as we have never seen a brisk watermelon. We should love to see them dashing about the place while buyers keenly demanded them, and found that they were not forthcoming. It shows a deplorable obstinacy on the part of the watermelon which we have never suspected. Of course, later on they became easier. Worn out, we suppose.

All this mucking about must naturally have its effect on the market habitués, and, so far as we can see, they are a pretty coarse lot.

For instance, a buyer never asks for anything; he always makes a strong demand for it. Not only this, but the demand varies. They probably stalk into the markets and bellow, 'We demand oranges!' or, varying it, 'Come across with the oranges!' or then again, 'Come out of that, and give us some oranges!' Is it any wonder that the oranges become firm and harden? Of course, these people have their troubles too. Only a couple of weeks ago 'the market was flooded with bananas.'

It was then a case of women and children first. Had the bottom not fallen. out of the market shortly after the flood, it is reasonable to suppose that buyers and sellers would still be baling the place out.

It will be plainly seen that, what with all this, and the cauliflowers moving steadily, onions falling, cabbages advancing, carrots active, and unsteady turnips staggering about the place, the market is no place for weaklings. Marketers die young.

Love and Kisses

Love!

What scenes are called up by the mere mouthing of the word! What scenes! What hellishing rows! A film which involves a fair amount of kissing has recently been banned by the Chief Commonwealth Censor. Not that that matters. He hasn't been properly kissed.

We have been kissed, ourself.

In our adolescent stages we were once so kissed that we ran around in circles for some days, and for weeks after that we walked about in a trance.

There was one ... older 'n us, she was – she said, 'Kizz muh!'

Got a half-nelson on us, she did, and they had to bring us brandy and undo our collar and use artificial respiration. Never been quite the same since. She was one of these tall, sinuous women who never seem to have any money.

Then there was a brunette. She was one who used to gradually look closer and closer into your eyes, until the back of your head hit the wall. Waggle her eyelashes on your neck and start the real business from the back of your ear and work round to the front of your face, by which time you had swooned away.

One way and another, we missed a lot of fun, swooning away.

Maisie – she was a nice girl. We should have smashed her teeth in about four times a week. She said she could only treat us as a sister would a brother. Used to kiss us on the forehead!

Asked her, in desperation, how long this sister business would be going on. She said, 'For ever!' and burst into tears.

So we told her that we had a sister, and strode off into the night.

We have been kissed by distant female relatives.

We have even been kissed by our wife.

She says, 'Whisky!'

'No! No! Dear!' we say, virtuously.

'Kiss me again' ... 'Brandy.'

We blush.

'You've had four brandies!'

We give in and confess to the four. What else can you do when you know that you've had twelve brandies?

Love, these days, gives us a pain in the small of the back. If anyone wants to censor kissing, we are on his side.

The Maoris rub noses instead of kissing, and our idea of Paradise is a place full of nose-less Maoris.

We are, of course, open to conversion ...

Pet Annoyances

Life, according to Professor Cason, of Rochester University, New York, is marred by 507 classifiable annoyances. He has compiled a list allotting a maximum of 30 marks for the supreme annoyance.

He gives 22 marks to 'Hair in the soup.' Flies are up near the front with 25 marks, while cockroaches are running a close second with 24, and 'dirty beds' romp home with 28 marks.

Speaking for ourself, we know the whole 507 of them. We travel in the same tram with him every morning.

He's a 'shunter,' among other things. A shunter is one of those chaps who, by slapping you in the chest, digging you in the ribs, breathing into your face, and talking right into your mouth, gradually gets you backing away until you finally finish up some 20 yards from the place where he first started to tell you his story.

If we had the courage, we'd give him just 1 mark – fair between the eyes.

Apart from this, local annoyances are fairly easy to classify.

First Class Annoyance, Grade A. – Being broke, 30 marks.

Going to work, 29 marks; the boss, 28; the assistant

boss, 27; inaudible and non-working telephones, 26; men who invented telephones, 25; stop-start-stop-start trams in rush hours, 24; dropping the bottle at 6.15 p.m. when it's too late to go back and get more, 23; traffic cops, 22; rainy weekends, 21; ... you see the idea?

All you have to do is to get about 3-cwt. of paper and a gross of pencils and start in making a list of the things that annoy you.

Professor Cason, who started this game, questioned 21,000 people over a period of several years. Probably they were too polite to tell him what really did annoy them most. But you needn't do this.

You'll find plenty to go on with. Especially if you start on Monday morning, after a wet week-end.

Can You Bite the Back of Your Own Neck?

To sit on your own lap! It seems an impossible feat. But that is what Ruth Chatterton does in 'The Right to Love.' She plays the daughter and mother. This achievement is due to the Dunning process, a new and remarkable discovery.

So there you are. But do we stop there? No! Science must march on.

We are now in the throes of discovering the Lower process, by means of which man will be enabled to take a running jump at himself.

What would his Neanderthal forefathers say to that?

Furthermore, the time is not far distant when Science will grant to man the inestimable boon of being able to bite himself on the back of the neck at any hour of the day or night!

In our laboratories – the very same one in which a young doctor, a martyr to science, gave himself freckles in order to study the effects – in our laboratories we are now gradually getting into shape the culminating triumph.

It is so big that we are almost afraid to give it to the world.

After years of experiment, we have almost perfected a process whereby a man can go through his own pockets while he is asleep!

This will make man practically self-contained and will do away with the necessity for marriage and probably wreck the social structure of our time.

But let there be no dismay. One must have a wife, because the machine will never be invented that can find your back stud.

Saying which, he strode thoughtfully back to his test-tubes.

Chivalry, Thou Art Not Dead

Though depression may still be here, chivalry is not dead. Probably because politeness costs nothing.

Abraham Wicks, taxi driver of this town, drove a well-dressed gentleman from the Quay to the Hotel Australia, the fare being 1/4.

'I'm afraid, I have not sufficient money,' said the fare. 'Will you accept stamps?'

And the taxi-man got five pennies and one shilling's worth of stamps. He took it with that innate politeness so popular with taxi-drivers.

Take our own experiences. We said to the driver, 'We are afraid we are stone, motherless, hearts-of-oak. Will you accept empty bottles, a pen-knife, and two dirty handkerchiefs?'

'Oui!' said the driver (an educated man). 'But I shall have to give you the change in spark-plugs.'

'It is well,' we said.

We turned to go, but the training of a thousand years drew us back.

'You have served us faithfully for the past ten minutes,' we said. 'If ever you need a reference, come out to La Perouse.'

We took off our left boot. 'Some little recognition of your service,' we said.

'Thank you, sir. Thank you!'

We stood on the steps of the Australia and watched him push his taxi back towards the rank. We are glad that it was mostly downhill.

The Bachelors' Guide to the Care of the Young

I have noticed with astonishment the absolute ignorance of bachelors in regard to the care of the young.

To begin at the beginning. It will be noticed in a fresh baby that it is of a pale, prawn-like color, and is bald and toothless, exhibiting all the evidences of senility. This is the usual thing, and the minder is not to be alarmed.

The first thing noticeable about the baby is the yowl. This must be stopped at all costs. There are various methods, but the principle to keep in mind is – at all costs. Watches are very good; a firm hold must be kept on the chain, however, as I have on two occasions lost a perfectly good watch through the child swallowing it.

This mania for swallowing and sucking things may be indulged to an almost unlimited extent. Door-knobs are excellent, though the holding of the baby to the knob is somewhat tiring. This may be overcome by unscrewing the hinges of the door and placing it in an accessible position.

Babies of an artistic nature or of practically any nature, may be left with a tin of stove-polish or a bottle of red ink or any other medium for an almost indefinite period.

In cases of persistent howling, a belt passed over the top of the head and buckled securely under the chin is an infallible remedy. This must be used only in extreme cases.

In handling, care must be taken that the baby is held in a more or less vertical position, the head being uppermost. The child at times has a tendency to jerk from the holder, and in the case of a beginner this may lead to disastrous results. Sticking-plaster and other first-aid appliances will be found very useful on these occasions, and a supply should always be kept on hand.

Where a baby has to be held for any length of time, a short loop of stout twine passed around the neck, and fastened to the wrist of the holder, will prevent contact with the floor.

Never allow a dog to lick the face of a baby as any number of diseases may be communicated, and in the case of a valuable dog, this is most serious and may lead to its loss, or, at the best, a falling-off of condition, and an absence of lustre in the coat.

On two or three occasions I have found the addition of about one-third of a cupful of rum to the feeding milk very effective. Only the best O.P. rum may be used, as babies are very delicately constituted internally. A better way is for the minder to have four or five cupfuls himself, when it will be found that an extraordinary number of ways of amusing the child will suggest themselves.

Should the little one inadvertently eat anything it shouldn't, thoroughly rinse or gargle the mouth with phenol, lysol, or any other good disinfectant.

In undressing the baby for the purposes of putting it to bed, bathing, etcetera, the beginner will find great difficulty in undoing the numerous buttons, tapes, and various other fastenings with which it is lashed.

An efficient and obvious method is to insert a penknife between the skin and the clothing and peel the mass off in one operation.

In bathing the child, never fill the bath right up, as it is only in exceptional cases that it will float. A cold shower and a brisk rub down with a stiff towel will have an invigorating and tonic effect.

In conclusion, a little helpful advice to the unwilling minder will not be amiss. Should you have been lured into minding a baby before, and wish to escape a second demand, a convincing excuse must be made. Lodge meetings and appointments, business or otherwise, are received with suspicion. By far the best is the statement that you feel your diphtheria coming back, and that you seem to be breaking out in funny red spots all over the body. This may be said in a conversational manner just as the request is about to be sprung. I have used this or something similar, for some time now, and it has never failed yet.

Let Us Be Ill

We have been lying in ambush for a long time, and at last a doctor has confessed that he is treating imaginary diseases with sham medicine.

One of our most cherished possessions was blood pressure. We went to see a doctor about it, and he sounded and plummeted us and said, 'Mm'm!' He then retired to his office and sharpened his pencil.

That was half a guinea.

He came back and wrote a lie, which started off, 'Mis X. 1/2/'32; R/ ... Sodi Chlor. grs xx.; Ext. Glycy. liq. m. XV. Mitte M&N pc.'

... Which meant a hot bath between meals, in water, and a complete change.

We were cured and were foully done out of a complaint which we had nursed for years and had got us a deal of sympathy while we had the opportunity of suffering.

An even dirtier trick is when you go to the studio suffering from all the symptoms of cancer, and the fool pounds you on the back and tells you you've been eating too much watermelon.

For all he knows you might have the acute appendicitis you first suspected.

There is even a book on Medical Judas-Prudence.

Our advice is to treat yourself.

Tell yourself to go for a long sea-trip, charge yourself 10/6, snap your fingers in your face, don't go for the long sea-trip, and pocket the half-guinea.

Better still – owe it to yourself for eight months.

Bananas in Bootees

'It would be extremely interesting to carry out experiments by covering bananas likely to mature during the winter months with bags.'

It would be interesting, but somewhat tedious, putting the little chaps into their bags. They're bound to grow out of them, and there's nothing looks more slovenly than a banana with an ill-fitting bag.

They look very chic in knitted bootees, but the question of expense must be considered.

It would be even more interesting to put galoshes on potatoes during the rainy season, while it would be positively thrilling to fit the watermelons with double-breasted coats.

We have recently been concentrating on beans.

It will be remembered that we were the first beaniarist to produce the Scarlet Runner. We trained it to run so fast that snails dropped exhausted in its tracks.

Perhaps in our zeal we overdid the thing.

Our last crop had to be picked by bean pickers on motor cycles.

We dabbled a little in marrows last season, but the ants were so annoying we had to blow up the one we hollowed out for a garage.

As a sideline we have been working on an odorless onion.

We have also planted a tomato which has not yet come up. Everything points to success.

The Very Latest in Fish Yarns
Just a Minute!

Grafton, Friday.
Six feet two inches long, and weighing 232 pounds, a
groper pulled a rowing-boat with three men in it
about the Clarence River, below Grafton, for 20
minutes before the fishermen were able to drag it
close enough to the boat to secure it with a piece of
wire through its gills.

Then there was the bait. A green prawn, weighing 180lb., including sinker, was cast off the rocks at Bondi and immediately swam off, taking with it the fisherman, his two companions, and the rocks.

Crashing into the Malolo (which sank immediately), the bait continued, until finally it was taken by a groper, which was first thought to be Tasmania.

Passing Africa, the three fishermen, who had been floating without an excuse between them on the rocks for five days, decided to haul in the line. The hook and sinker had gone.

The long swim back to Bondi left them exhausted, and a kindly native revived them with a few rums.

Ultimately they arrived home. And their wives said, 'FISHING!'

And a few other things.

(Don't miss our next issue. Every week-end!)

Rabbits, If You Like

Our rabbit has died.

A bit of a blow after what the National Council of Women said.

We had great expectations of him, because he was an Angora rabbit, and we expected to clip wool off him every three months, according to directions, and export it to cardigan jacket manufacturers.

Still, we learned a fair bit about rabbits, while he lived. The Angora rabbit inhabits the mountain fastnesses of Angora, boring holes into the faces of precipices with its back feet.

This, so that if the rabbit should wish to leave the hole, it need not turn round. The hole is known as a burrow. The difference between a burrow and a borrow is that when one wants to burrow one makes a hole.

When you borrow you're already in a hole.

Obvious, of course, but we thought we'd point it out to you.

We knew a rabbit once, his name was Alphonso, after the King of Spain, who recently aspirated – which is a mos' Spainful subject.

He (the rabbit) used to dog, or rabbit, our footsteps wherever we went. Its fleece was white as snow. It followed us to school one day. We used it to chase ferrets.

It was a sad day for us when four actors came along (and wanted a rabbit's foot each, for luck). It was bad luck for the rabbit.

We made a cardigan jacket out of the remains. From the experience we gained on that occasion, we advise all future rabbit ranchers to take the meat part out of the rabbit before making a jacket of the fur.

And another thing. One rabbit doesn't go fur enough.

Now, warren know about that!

About Frogs

A Brisbane frog arrived at Mascot on the tail-plane of the Brisbane mail plane yesterday morning.

This is probably the longest hop ever taken by a frog.

The frog is a strange animal which lives in creeks and croaks.

It also lives on water and hops.

One frog is spawn every minute. The stages of the frog are interesting to be interested in.

First the spawn. Then the rod, tadpole, or perch. Then the frog on its log in the bog. (Poetry.)

We have the bull-frog. The cow-frog and the calf-frog were last seen at the battle of Blenheim (1345, A.D.)

The tadpole is an apprentice frog. Tadpoles born in May are Maypoles.

The barberspole is a frog which comes out in red, white, and blue stripes when fully matured. It costs 6d. in most places, or 9d. with a hot towel.

In France, people eat frogs – fifty million Frenchmen can't be wrong.

Eat more frogs. Of course, in the case of there being a death in France since time of writing, there is a possibility of forty-nine million nine hundred and ninety-nine thousand nine hundred and ninety-nine Frenchmen being misled.

But let it be here stated that the frog which arrived on the Brisbane mail plane was a bull frog, because it was a mail frog.

And if it wasn't a bull frog that rode on the mail plane, it must have been toad.

Lowerism

We have been told to write a limerick. We once lost pounds on a horse of that name, which maybe has something to do with our failure.

There was a young man from the West,

(We don't come from the West, but who cares about that?)

Was depressed and depressed and depressed
And depressed and depressed
And depressed and depressed
And depressed and depressed and depressed.

Drinks with a Kick in Them

The President of the Housewives' Association says that she does not believe in cocktail drinking, and could if necessary, produce a drink with a 'kick' in it, from fruit.

Anticipating, we have evolved a few recipes to suit all tastes.

BANANA FLUTTER – Take one banana, slice, and put into glass. Take half a coconut and beat it into a stiff froth. Mix briskly and serve. The 'kick' is obtained by standing on one foot on the skin of the banana and leaning forward while pouring the drink down the back of the neck.

Then we have the FLYING MULE – Take half-dozen raspberries, being careful to remove the seeds, also the sound. Mash lightly with hammer. Mix with little ice-water, and add seeds slowly, one at a time, until you are so thirsty that you'd drink anything. Now take a red-hot nail, and dip it smartly into the mixture, removing it almost immediately. Drink nail.

THE WATERMELON WHOOPEE – Take one large watermelon, cut in half. Hollow out one half and place contents in wash-basin. Save seeds from other half. Place in wash-basin one small cup of gramophone needles, half-pint of sulphuric acid. Drink before bottom falls out of wash-basin.

A similar mixture is the HANGOVER BLUES. The watermelon is put into the wash-basin as before, but covered with crushed ice. The hollowed-out portion is then quarter-filled with crushed ice and placed over the head, taking care to pull it well down over the forehead. The face is then laid gently in the wash-basin.

It will be seen from the above recipes that the uses of fruit as a drink are practically unlimited. Furthermore, most fruit is full of vitamines.

These need not worry the hostess, however, as they can easily be detected by the small holes in the outside of the skin, and this part can be cut out.

And don't forget – all these drinks have a kick.

The careful hostess should warn her guests of this danger.

Wagers that are Worth Making

An Easy Way to Get Rid of Undesirables

About this golfer who is going to play golf from Brisbane to Adelaide, via Sydney and Melbourne – he is not allowed to touch the ball with his hands or feet unless with special permission.

We suppose he will be allowed to bowl it along with his forehead occasionally. It wouldn't do the ball any harm and might do the golfer a lot of good.

We often wonder who lays all these wagers. We are going to be one of them. We shall challenge our landlord to push a wheelbarrow across Australia, hopping on one foot. And when he comes back and puts his barrow wearily down outside the vacant house the next-door neighbour will say: 'Lower? He left here a week ago.'

And we shall go to the Taxation Commissioner and say to him: 'Excuse me, but would you mind bowling a hoop around the world for a bet?'

Then we would go along to Parliament House and say: 'We bet you aren't game to sit on a two hundred foot pole for about eleven years.'

And when we had got them all sitting on poles, and pushing barrows, and walking from Sydney to

Bechuanaland, and slipping on banana-skins from Perth to Redfern, we would sit down, fold our hands one within the other, and begin to enjoy life.

Girls, How to Acquire 'It'!

Free Beauty Secrets

Attention, girls!

Just a few words on how to use your lipstick and face powder.

Mr Ernest Young, a London educationist, has said, 'I implore art teachers to teach girls to use powder and lipstick artistically and correctly.'

He shall not implore in vain.

First of all it is necessary to have a face, with a mouth in it. The face should be washed and, if the means are at hand, dried. A piece of well-chalked string is then tied to one ear, stretched across the face to the other ear, and then given a slight flip with the fingers.

This will result in a white chalk-line across the face, which will give the position for the rouge on the cheeks. The rouge may be applied with a small mop or a trowel, care being taken to scoop any surplus out of the ears.

The face is now taken across the dressing room and pushed into the powder. With the face buried, blow vigorously, thus distributing the powder all over the face and neck. Some cream the face before powdering. This gives a nice stucco effect.

Now take the left hand and slide it down the face

until you come to an aperture. This is the mouth.

Work the lipstick into whatever shape the mouth is to be, and press it on while still plastic.

When pencilling the eyebrows always use an indelible pencil. Nothing is more untidy than a girl who, while pushing her hair back, has wiped one of her eyebrows off. Those lucky girls who can yawn naturally should add the weeniest touch of rouge to the tonsils.

That will be all for the present, girls.

Remember – Art, and plenty of it.

Has A Wooden Expression

If an investor in the State Lottery won the first prize 200 times in succession in one year, he would be able to pay most of the £2,000,000 which is lost to Sydney annually in damage done by borers. This would be very jolly of him.

A much better idea would be to get rid of the borers.

This may be done by filling up each hole as it is made. The borer makes another hole, and so one proceeds until the frustrated borer goes raving mad and bores itself to death.

The borer is also known as the furniture beetle (not to be confused with the lounge lizard, which lives entirely on upholstery and cigarettes), and may be recognised by its wooden expression and vegetarian outlook on life.

In the case of a virile and energetic borer, specimens of which may frequently be found at the Stock Exchange and at various golf clubs, the same methods of extermination are applied as in the first instance.

A strong-minded furniture beetle will not go mad after having its exits plugged up. It will keep on boring until the article of furniture crashes to the ground and the pest is crushed beneath the ruins.

It w-- p-ea-e many to -earn that for the -arger furniture beet-e- vario-s reme-ie- have been devi-e-. Of

th-s- we mention two. One i- to -mear the article with jam
in which is mixe- a -ittle -trychnine, an- the other, to -en-
a ferret in after them.

At this stage the borers were in complete control.

By Gripes!

It has come to my notice, said he, tugging furiously at his moustache, that the Seamen's Union is being white-anted. White ants are responsible for the holding-up of ships. The enormous strength of these little creatures can be approximately guessed at. It is nothing to hear of them holding up two or three ships at a time.

The headline in the 'S.M. Herald,' 'White-anting the Seamen,' sent a thrill down my back (and I have a small mole in the middle of my back, making it much harder for the thrill, especially when I have my tight singlet on which only goes to show you); and the thought of the poor seamen, riddled with white ants, decayed inside, although looking all right on the exterior, and having to have their feet painted with creosote fills me with dismay.

The methods of the white ant are strange but good. It inserts a small hole in the furniture with its beak and burrows into the wood, kicking the sawdust out with its back feet. Any householder coming home late at night and finding a heap of sawdust alongside the kitchen table, should say, 'Ha! Ha! White ants!' Of course, it is not compulsory to say this, the 'Ha! Ha!' may be left out if you are not a bachelor, but anyhow, immediate action must be taken.

Carefully smash the table with an axe. Grasp the ant by the wrist and lead it out into the open. Gently stun it and put it on one side.

Peel an onion. Squeeze two nutmegs. Stir briskly.

Belt the ant a few times in the face with an anvil. This will teach it a lesson. A simpler method is to carve a piece out of the piano and bait a trap. White ants like pianos. They have musical ears.

Learn to play a white ant in six easy lessons! Send no money. We trust you! If not satisfied, send ant back!

READ THIS! 'Dear Sir, — Three weeks ago I was a social disaster. All I could do was to stay in the kitchen and wash the glasses. Then I bought a white ant with musical ears. Since then I have been invited to go to all sorts of places. I have even been invited to go to Blazes. People take notice of me now. There is always a scatter when I come along with my ant. You may use this letter as you like. I enclose photo of myself with your white ant. The one on the left is me. — Yrs. truly, L. Frobisher, Laverton, Q.'

But to get back to it.

The ant, scenting the chunk of piano from afar, plods doggedly into the trap. The rest is easy if the trap knows its work.

A more subtle and fiendish method which makes the Royal Society for the Prevention of Cruelty to Ants, wake up in a cold sweat at two o'clock in the morning, is the billiard ball trick.

The ant is pushed into a room, in which there is one billiard ball. It is impossible to nibble a billiard ball. Try it yourself.

That way lies madness. Which is exactly what happens.

The frustrated ant gnaws and gnaws and gnaws and gnaws and gnaws (I get paid by the line for this) and gnaws and gnaws and gnaws and gnaws, and what happens? Nothing. This preys on the ant's mind until it becomes hopelessly mental, and is carried away frothing at the mouth.

Which is very sad, and I hope I have not upset you.

The Terrors of Wealth

Half a million germs lurk on a pound note.

This has been discovered by a scientist. Probably he borrowed the pound. This means 250,000 germs stroll about a ten-shilling note, and 125,000 germs are waiting to pounce from five shillings – 25,000 germs on a shilling! Heavens, do you realise what peril you live in?

Could any man with a spark of humanity in his soul lend a man two bob, knowing that it carried with it 50,000 germs, mostly unclassified.

Every citizen in this country who is in possession of a pound-note is a menace.

The Government has done its best. It has taxed us 25,000 germs in every half million. It has taxed us countless germs annually. But is it enough?

NO! (Applause.)

It has come to our notice that a well-known identity has been walking about our city, defying our Government and laughing in the faces of the police, carrying a pound-note in his left-hand pocket.

This man is a carrier.

Hold him!

Stop him!

Recall the Governor!

Do something. Hooray!

Ambition and Success

Many and various are the roads to success, and not all of them are up-hill, though the roads down which one can toboggan are hard to find, and for the most part private.

The methods of the successful differ. There is the romantic method.

The humble workman marries the boss's daughter, after which the boss falls into the machinery, and the hero is set for life.

Then there is the man who rises to the occasion. This generally happens when the mine is caving in, and all the workmen except one flee for their lives. The one left holds the mine up with his back until assistance comes, and then collapses into the arms of the mine-owner, with the words, 'I have done my best.' The mine-owner may reply that he has seen it done better, but usually the man is promoted.

* * *

By far the best-advertised method, and one highly recommended by numerous moral journals, is the 'humble striver.'

The idea of this method is that no matter how lowly

your job, humbly strive to be a pastmaster at it.

Which recalls the story of the gutter-sweeper in a far country, who decided to be the best gutter-sweeper in the world. For years he swept as no other man could sweep, until one day, the Grand Hokum, going through the streets, passed the remark: 'My word, that gutter is clean! Who cleaned it?'

And the Deputy-Commissioner for Gutters replied: 'Sire, I believe it was the slave, Bill Smith.'

And the Grand Hokum said: 'Has he a cat?'

And the Chief Broom Stacker answered:— 'Yea sire, a beaut!'

'Then make him Lord Mayor!' said the Grand Hokum, and passed on.

You see how the good and faithful worker is rewarded!

* * *

Then again, there was the nut-screwer who worked in an automobile factory, and didn't even have a name, but was called 'Number 74.'

All he did was to screw a nut on a steel plate when it was thrown at him.

And they were thrown at him at the rate of twenty-five a minute.

You would think with so much spare time on his hands that the nut-screwer would get careless and discontented.

But not Number 74!

He set out to be the best nut-screwer in the factory, and took steel plates home with him after his work was done, and got his wife to throw them at him, and he practised far into the night.

And as time went on, the foreman noticed him, and told the chief foreman about it. And the chief foreman told the sub-manager of the department, and so it went on until at last the Great Managing Director was brought to see the nimble nut-screwer at work.

'How long,' he said to Number 74, 'have you been screwing nuts?'

'Fifteen years, sir.'

'You are a good nut-screwer?'

'I am the best nut-screwer in the world, sir.'

And the great man said 'H'm!' and walked away.

And Number 74 drew a deep breath and shook hands with himself, and wondered if he would be made a director straight away, or if he would have to spend a short time as sub-manager.

And later, the foreman came to him and said, 'I have a message for you.'

And Number 74 smiled.

'As you are the best nut-screwer in the world,' said the foreman, 'I am directed to tell you that you will be kept on the nut-screwing staff indefinitely, provided that you are of good behaviour, and don't slacken off, or get sick, or cheeky, or anything like that.'

And Number 74 said, 'Thank you,' very feebly, and fell on his spanner and died.

And they threw his useless body out of the way, and engaged another nut-screwer.

Which shows you that virtue is its own reward.

Cruel Tactics of the Emu

Sad news comes from Wangrabelle.

It seems that emus chase the sheep and kill them by repeatedly jumping on their backs. They do the same thing to pigs.

It is supposed that the emus do this out of a spirit of sportive destructiveness as they do not further mutilate the animals after killing them.

Anyone who knows anything at all about emus must know that it's not the fault of the emus. They have nothing else to do. They are merely emusing themselves.

As an emuologist who has made a close study of emus for many years, we say without fear of contradiction that if the sheep or pig, as the case may be, would only keep steady, the emu would not have to keep jumping on and off.

Experiments have proved beyond all doubt that a pig or sheep once jumped on begins to wobble.

The Emu Research Society, of which we are the founder, in combination with the Be-Kind-To-Emus League, has jumped on the backs of 3425 pigs, and a similar number of sheep in the course of experiment, the animals being kindly lent by owners of piggeries and sheeperies.

In every case the result was fatal, this may be accounted for by the fact that there is a total of 132 in the experimental party, and even though the investigators jumped one at a time, the animal selected soon weakened and was ultimately flattened out.

Emus cannot be curbed. An emu which was born in our own home and fed by our own hand, returned to its wild state at the end, and after laying an egg in the jardiniere, kicked the back out of the fireplace.

The solution lies in breeding stronger sheep. More powerful pigs. Given the right physique, look what a saving in freights would be effected if farm produce could swim to the London market.

There's something wrong with the backs of our sheep. The knees of our pigs are not all that they should be. We ought to look into the backs and knees of our sheep and pigs. In the meantime, you leave our emus alone.

Losers and Lottery

Interviewed by our Exceptional Correspondent, one of the losers of the State Lottery was somewhat shy.

Asked what he intended to do, the almost frantic loser said that he intended to buy an hotel. It was his intention to buy it one beer at a time.

Mrs K., of Lakemba, admits that had an 8 been a 5 and the 31 been a 13, she would have been very close to a 10/- prize.

Mr L., of Maroubra, has decided to buy an orange and settle down.

'I have always had a longing to travel,' said the loser of the third prize. 'I think I will take a trip around the bathroom.' Mr L. will be accompanied by his son, Master M.

'I am very glad – not for myself alone – that our syndicate failed to draw a prize in the lottery,' said Mrs J. 'The losing of the prize delights me, as all the rest of the syndicate are very annoyed.'

The general consensus of opinion is that there is a hole in the barrel, and that Mr Whiddon is in the pay of the Soviet Government.

The Butchers' Picnic

Butchers shut up their chops yesterday and went to a picnic. It's about time they had a spell.

It's time the abattoirs had a spell too, only they're so hard to spell.

It was yesterday we were sent for a pound of steak, and given 1/8, and we had to get sixpennorth of ham instead – the change was ours.

The butchers had their picnic just for the change. That's the only reason we ever volunteer to go to the butchers'. Just for the change.

You get interested in butchers when they butcher to a lot of trouble.

How many of us know one slab of steak from another? There are the bladebone steaks, porterhouse steaks, Adrian Knox Stakes, Cantala Stakes, and kid-stakes, which you only dish up as a last resource.

Take chops. A chop is merely a steak with a bone in it. If a sausage had a backbone and a bulging forehead, it would be a chop.

Dare say there are any number of sausages taking correspondence courses, hoping to become chops.

A butcher, kidneys wife, may be a high liver, but he lives according to his lights; it's a heart life.

Sheep's Head cannot be found on the atlas, and altogether, the butcher is worthy of his steal.

Any man who takes a holiday now is mad; but a butcher, his job is skewer.

Saying which, he fell on his gherkins and abandoned the butchering business.

Which was only meet.

Recomember! The butcher was the man who put the 'laughter' into 'slaughter.'

Let him get thick on his hollow-day.

Watchman, What of the Wife?

We have often wondered who those people were who seem to have nothing else to do but watch men digging the road up or working down holes. They are private detectives. They watch.

Every morning in the Agony Column is the information.

'Detective Agency. Persons watched from 5/-. Lowest charges. Easy terms.' One detective agency says it 'will go anywhere.' Further down in the column, someone else offers to watch people for 4/6. There is competition even in the watching business.

When watching falls as low as 4/6 a go, it seems a shame not to have someone watched. For instance, the Boss is seen going out. The detective (engaged by the whole staff) is immediately put on the job. He reports, 'Boss seen entering club at 1.15 p.m. Having Turkish bath.' This, of course, means at least three hours off for the staff.

Then, 'Boss leaving club at 4.20 p.m. Seems to be in bad temper.'

All work like mad.

With increased business, watching costs could be lowered to the point where even the smallest purse could afford a little investigating.

Little difficulties would arise, naturally.

'I've had a very tiring day,' you would say on arriving home.

'Oh!' the wife would reply. 'Is that why you spent 1/4 in the public bar of Swamper's Hotel, on the corner of Sussex Street and Moore Park, remaining there from 5.32 p.m. until 5.59 ½ p.m. on the 24th inst.? ... while I've been slaving away in the house ...'

'Stop!' you'd reply, producing your notes. 'You can't tell me you've been slaving when I have definite information to say that you were leaning on the fence, 27th paling from the left, standing on a bucket, marked X in the diagram, from 2.10 p.m. until 4.15 of the same date, discussing ...'

It would be goodo, if one could get someone to watch the detective.

'Call Me Aggie'
Hooray for the Dean of Canterbury!

He had said: 'I am no blooming good as Dean of Canterbury. That's why I don't wear gaiters. Give me a run for my money. Call me Dick Sheppard. Give me your right hand, invite me to your socials, let me be a pal.'

That's the stuff to give the troops! With such a precedent, any minute now we're expecting an announcement from Mr Scullin on the same lines.

'I'm no good as Prime Minister and Federal Treasurer. That's why you don't wear socks. Give me a run for your money. Call me Jimmy. Give me your right hand, left hand, and both feet. Make a pal of me. Put kisses on the bottom of your income tax returns. Invite me to your funeral.'

But of course, it is in the church that this democracy will make the biggest difference.

You will be greeted at the church door by the Dean, and he will say, 'Well, well! If it's not old Bill! How the hell are you? Haven't seen you for years. Come inside. The boys are just having an ace-pot for the last, and then we'll start the service.'

It might even catch on when the Mayoress of Tasmania or some other distinguished lady attends the official opening of the Girls' Christian Reform Guild in the parish hall. (They have a new parish hall in Tasmania on the site where the old Mechanics' Institute used to be.)

She will probably enter on a scooter and yell, 'Whoopee, girls! Smoke up, don't mind me. Whaddyer think of me new garters. Trot out the beer and call me Aggie.'

The thing will probably receive a serious setback when the Dean of Newcastle slaps one of the local miners on the back and says, 'Hullo, you old cow! How's the old coal-stained body?'

The miner will hand him one and the Dean will go out for the count, and some more.

Democracy is all right as a hobby, but you can't come that stuff on us blokes.

The Napkin or the Lapkin

The table napkin, alias the serviette, has a little brother – the Lapkin. The lapkin is the American idea of a non-skid table napkin. Instead of being square, it's rectangular. Americans now sit down to a square meal with a rectangular napkin all round.

For some time we have been considering the patenting of the 'strapkin,' which fastens under the legs, also the 'grapkin,' which consists of a water-proof cape, fastening at the throat and buckling at the ankles.

Sufficient attention is not paid to safety, apart from etiquette, at the dinner table.

For instance, on Sunday, a man had a watermelon seed removed from his ear by the local chemist. We suggest, with some hesitancy, that he should be more careful when eating melon.

The ordinary method of drinking soup is also highly dangerous.

It runs down the chin, corroding the front stud, and setting up gangrene of the Adam's apple.

A straw or glass tube would be easier, safer, and less wasteful, and it could be even sucked through a tin whistle, which would give far more beautiful effects, properly fingered, than the ordinary spoon soloist could hope to produce.

Why not strapped elbows?

You know, when you're cutting your steak the fork suddenly drags it apart, your elbow hits the next diner just over the heart, and he's out to it.

If you're standing up (supposing the steak is extra tough), you're liable to knock a man's brains out.

But is all this improvement really worth anything?

The American lapkin may stay on the lap, but we prefer the old type which always falls on to the floor and gets mixed up with your boot-lace, and gives you an opportunity, when recovering it, of seeing whose feet you've been flirting with.

And which of the ladies have their shoes off ... 'n jazz garters ...

Taking everything into consideration, we think they're better, square.

Money Box as Bait

*Great excitement was caused in Port Macquarie on
Thursday night, when Mr R. G. Davidson landed a
56 lb. jewfish from the verandah of his residence,
facing the harbour.*
*Before retiring for the night, Mr Davidson set his
bait, the alarm being his little girl's money-box
fastened to the line.*

This is not the first jewfish to be landed with a money-box bait. Nor is it the first one to be caught from a harbour-side verandah.

We once baited a set line with a money box and the jewfish, an old depositor weighing 10st. 11lb., fell for it, and the verandah was towed 11 miles out to sea.

We shall never forget it. It was a rough night, and the horizon was entirely obscured by the head of the jewfish and a few clouds.

A few words passed between the haggard crew on the verandah. There was only one of us who knew how to steer a verandah. That was me.

'Haul in on the awnings!' we shouted. 'Belay the cane chair abaft!' This was done – and not a moment too soon. The fish turned and came racing towards us.

'Shift the verandah about a mile and a half to the left!' we bellowed. Too late. The fish landed on the verandah, spat out the money-box, and said: 'Me – with £35 in the Government Savings Bank and you toss me a money-box with 1/9 in it! ...'

We remembered no more until we found ourself on the beach with a voice saying, 'Drink this.'

Oh, to hear that voice again!

It may sound absurd to you, but we can show you the place where it got away.

If You Buy This Elephant You've Got a Hide

Things must be very bad in Hobart. They are selling their elephant. He is selling his elephant, you are selling your elephant, we are selling our elephant, thou has put thine elephant up for sale (Grammar).

As proof of which, here's the advertisement: —

CITY OF HOBART
FOR SALE – ONE MALE ELEPHANT

13 years old, very docile and accustomed to giving rides to children. Any reasonable offer will be considered. Town Hall, HOBART.

W. A. BRAIN, Town Clerk.

Some say, on the one hand, that Tasmania is trying to pay off its deficit by selling its elephant.

Others, on the one hand left to them, say that it is a political move, that it is a white elephant, and Lang wants it.

The whole situation is intriguing and needs looking into by people like us who were born among elephants.

The very fact that the elephant lives in the Town Hall

is interesting.

That the elephant gives rides to children links it up with our Uncle Ernest, and must be very interesting to zoologists. And our Uncle Ernest didn't look a bit like an elephant. Nature is marvellous.

Train Turtles for Profit

Wanted, supplies Live Tortoise, immed. deliv.

We have been doing a bit of wavering, but we have decided that we cannot part with our 5000 tortoises.

We know each one of them by name. When we call they gallop up and eat out of our hand. In the case of a dead-heat between two tortoises, they eat out of both hands.

This to save bickering.

Then there were our turtles. They got in among the tortoises. We had to make separate pens for the turtises and tortles which were the unfortunate outcome.

We had a go at mating tortoises with hedgehogs, in order to produce tortoise-shell brushes, but this was a failure.

We had a frightful lot of trouble. There were the tortoises that turned turtle on us. As we said before, we knew the titles of our total turtles. There is nothing more affectionate than a turtle.

Their coats are so warm, and if you don't belt them in the face they'll do you no harm, as the old nursery rhyme says.

We strongly advise readers to take up turtles or tortoises as a hobby or profession.

Of course, it is difficult to take up a turtle as a tortoise, but the shearing season is between July and September, and the average torsle should yield about five dressing-table sets to the season.

This is about all we care to divulge about tortisels. Further information will be supplied on receipt of 10d. in stamps.

Opposition for Sydney Ferries

There is a ferry boat to be sold at auction on Tuesday.

We shall never forget the last ferry boat we bought.

Carried away in a frenzy of bidding, we found it knocked down to us at £9/10/-.

'Take it away,' said the auctioneer.

Having had some nautical experience, we knew what to do. A bag of coal cost us 4/6 or something. It was the work of a moment to stoke the fires.

Then, dashing up to the bridge, we rang the bell for 'Slow ahead.' Dashing down to the engine-room just in time to hear the bell, we put her on to 'Slow ahead.'

Tearing back to the bridge, we suddenly remembered that we hadn't cast-off, and immediately rushed to the lower deck in our capacity as deck-hand, and discovered that the hawser was under too great a strain to cast off. We hurled ourself up on the bridge and rang down the order, 'Stop. Slow astern.'

Leaping frenziedly to the engine-room, we then put her astern, dashed out of the engine-room, and cast off the mooring ropes. From there back to the bridge and our position as captain was merely a matter of agility.

By this time the coal had run out. We spun the wheel 14 times, failing, however, to rest on a winning number, and thus losing a box of chocolates.

We finished up adrift in the open sea. The boat sank and we were drowned with all hands – both of them.

This concluded our nautical career, and we are lucky to be able to tell the tale, drowned as we are.

————————

(This venture was a distinct loss to Mr Lower. Our accountant has analysed the position with the following result: —

    Depreciation of boat £9 10 0
    Cost of coal..0 4 6
    Fare paid at turnstile by Mr Lower ....<u>0 0 4</u>
    Total £9 14 10

Against this the sum of 4d., fare received by Captain Lower, must be offset. Net loss was, therefore, £9/14/6.

Mr Lower' s claim for expenses totalling this amount has been unanimously rejected.)

Perils of the Bathtub

What's a bath between friends? Nothing but a hollow porcelain division. Who invented baths? Some dirty cow.

Only dirty people bathe, as the Prophet hath said. Those who are not dirty, and yet bathe, do it out of pure flashness.

These thoughts are engendered by the recent law enacted by the Home Minister of Poland, wherein it is enacted (we like 'wherein it is enacted'; it has a partly gold watch-chained, bald-headed sound about it) that every Pole must bathe at least once a month.

Those under 10 and over 60 are exempt, also those possessing their own bathrooms, which it is presumed, are used.

Bathrooms in Poland are sufficient evidence in a case of Rex v. Perspiration.

Some similar action is needed in Australia. Such as:—

Act 79B, sub-section K2, Z1, relating to bathing of bodies: 'Be it heretofor whereas'd that inasmuch & so to speak, any person or persons turning on showers between or about the months of May, June, July, & standing near shaving cabinets, well away from showers, & saying, 'Br-r-r-r!' & singing "Annie Laurie" afterward coming out of bathroom, or rooms, & saying that there is nothing like a cold shower to freshen one up, shall be fined a maximum of £10 or a fortnight. God Save King.'

This will be one of the planks of the new Ruination Party, of which we have the honour of being president.

Any man who does more than bathe his eyes in this weather should be in a monastery. And anyhow, what advantage has the bather?

He comes from his cold shower, blue, numb, speechless. At his office he says, 'My word, the shower was cold this morning!'

And the man who wiped his eyes on a wet sponge says, 'One of the toughest surfs I've experienced this winter. All the Icebergs agreed.'

Let there be signs put up in all bathrooms similar to those on various beaches, 'Any person bathing here does so at his own risk.'

S.O.S.: Not, Shiver Our Skins – but Save Our Soap.

Men have been known to slip on a cake of soap and break their necks.

Be warned.

Let's Become Purer

Purity is rapidly becoming fashionable, thanks to Mr Norman Lindsay.

People who previously objected to it are now viewing it tolerantly. In Michigan, they aim to ban anything that tends to make vice more attractive and virtue a back number. Films must have no bedroom scenes, no bathroom scenes, no scanty clothing scenes, no demonstrations of passionate love, and no scenes of bloodshed or violence.

We look forward to the times when there will be no bathrooms, or if there are, when they are hermetically sealed and are referred to, when it is impossible to refrain from mentioning them, as the 'B.'

Soap, in these happy times, on account of its close association with the naked flesh, will be referred to as 'S,' and will be sold in packets labelled 'Dog Biscuits.' When retiring to the 'B.R.' (bedroom), the pure-minded man will not clothe himself scantily, but rather don an overcoat, and having locked the door, stand up in the wardrobe and go to sleep.

Demonstrations of passionate love will be confined to hand-shaking, and then only under proper supervision.

Violence and bloodshed will not be permitted except

in surgeries and dental parlors.

As for women – women will not be permitted at all.

Or perhaps they might be kept in compounds, wearing long chaff-bag coverings and stove-pipe leggings.

Anything calculated to arouse the baser passions, such as a knife and fork, will be used only by people of repute. Square plates of course. We can never look on a round plate without blushing at its curves.

If any reader can think of any other improvements, we will be glad to put them into effect, or ban them, or burn and prohibit and disinfect them.

We get a sensual pleasure out of banning things, and pure minds are full of things to ban.

Men Must Pay Heavily to be Beautiful

Doddering into the swellest barber's saloon in
town, we fell into a chair and said:
'Make us look human.'
'This is not a surgery,' replied the barber kindly.

Then we said, 'Shave us, shampoo, face massage, violent-ray, and de-blackhead us. We are in your hands.'

So he started. Right here we want to say that if ever you want the ravages of time and the effects of high living and low morals eradicated from the countenance, or face, do what we did.

It will only cost you about 25/- if you get out alive.

The shave, with eleven hot towels and three varieties of face cream. The hair-cut with the electric tooth-drill; the shampoo – these are mere preliminaries.

The hair is dried with hot air, both electrical and human.

Then starts the face massage. You are oiled, creamed, and bleared.

An electrical exasperator is wheeled up to your side. The operator turns the thing on, and you immediately get heebie-jeebies in the face.

You then disappear from human ken beneath a swathe of hot towels. The operator then goes away, presumably to the races or to have lunch.

After many years, during which your whole life passes before you, the towels are taken away and pink mud is rubbed, slapped, and pounded into your face.

Hydrochloric acid, or something more fierce, is poured on to you. Cream, oil – a final belt in the cheek, and you are massaged.

The violent-ray we took without anaesthetic. It consists of a swarm of starving ants with important appointments in your cerebral crannies.

Twice we nearly escaped, but we were brought back, giggling, with our tonsorial robes bedraggled, but still furled tightly around the neck.

We were given smelling salts, and a towel soaked in Florida water to suck.

Then we were manicured. Let us draw a curtain over this. We were thrown out of the manicure parlor. Nice girl, though.

And so back to the office, walking mincingly into the lift, asking the draivah to draive slowleh so as not to disturb ouah part.

Smelling strongly of Ashes of Chlorafleurs, we found we were most unwelcome. Our peaches and cream complexion was lost in our hasty retreat from the sub-editor's room to the lift.

N.B. – The lift driver has since had the elevator insectibaned.

Be Careful with Babies

Babies are in again.
World-known residents of Hollywood are having
them. Actually wheeling them around in a languid
perambulator.

Must be very awkward for fashionable celebrities with a first baby. It is in a spirit of kindness that we proffer instruction and advice, which follow:—

The top part of the baby is the part with the knob on it.

The ends which wave about are the legs.

It is not generally known that the baby must be held knob part up if the thing is to make any progress.

Babies on the bottle should be taught to use an opener at about three months. The label should be removed, so that the child will not form any prejudices against a certain brand which may affect him in later life.

At about six months chewing should commence, either on a bone ring or on the doctor's bill. Things being as they are, we recommend the doctor's bill, because a bone ring is just about finished in two years.

At two years the child's left leg should be tightly lashed to its left ear and rapidly whirled around. This will give it a good idea of. what constitutes a good citizen and taxpayer.

It will probably kill the kid, but everything is for the best.

Don's Boyhood Friends

It's marvellous the number of people who knew Don Bradman when he was a small boy in short trousers.
We met approximately 158 of them yesterday.

They told us: 'I used to say to young Don, "Don, you keep on the way you're going and some day you'll play for Australia." I could SEE that the boy was a born batsman ...' etc.

Plain bunk, that's all it is. Now when we knew young Don, WE used to say to him, 'Don, my boy, you keep on the way you're going ...'

As a matter of fact, we told the tramguard about it, sitting in the front seat on the way to Watson's Bay.

The driver nearly ran over four pedestrians, and the conductor forgot to collect our fare, thus allowing us a profit of 5d.

We were in the Court the other day when the murderer was asked if he had anything to say before being sentenced to death.

'Yes, Judge,' he replied. 'I think that Woodfull and Bradman are two of the greatest cricketers in history.'

Whereupon the whole Court cheered madly, and he was let off with a fine, the solicitors waiving costs. We even heard a rumour that members of the Union Club were kicking each other's hats around the billiard room.

There was a man sacked yesterday from a large Sussex Street warehouse, and pausing at the door, he said: 'Anyhow, I think we'll win this Test.'

So the boss said: 'Bring that man back. He's got brains. We can't afford to lose men like that.'

But it doesn't always work.

We got home pretty late last night, and thinking to get in first, said: 'What do you think! Bradman's 215 umpty not out!'

'Who is this Bradman?' she said, and while we were recovering, 'Anyhow, I don't wish to hear about your drunken friends. Two hundred and umpty not out! Why, YOU! You're only 30, and you're always out!'

What's a man to do with a woman like that?

Women have no sense of values.

Trout Season Now Open for Silver Fishermen

The trout season is now open. This reminds us of fish. There is a lot of thrills to be got out of fishing, though not much fish. We once struggled for nearly half an hour with a salmon, which only weighed about a pound. The label was torn to pieces, and the tin was dented in two places before we got him.

There are other ways of getting fish, even more strenuous.

Rock fishing, for instance. We don't recommend it unless you get paid by the hour. A man might waste half a ton of rocks before he hits one fish.

Then there's rod fishing. All right if you've got a good eye, and are a fairly straight shot with the rod.

Line fishing? Well, we know a fair amount about line fishing.

We have a line.

Some of us experts use a float instead of a sinker. We are not in favour of this. With a decent sinker, you at least have a chance of stunning the fish. Even if you don't catch the fish on the forehead with the sinker, there is always the possibility that the fish will swallow the thing, and die of lead poisoning.

Dynamiting is unsportsmanlike and uneconomical.

The procedure is to force the dynamite down the throat of the fish, and light the fuse. Throw the fish away and run like blazes.

The only fault in this method is that it does not do the fish much good. It sort of permanently cures it of being a fish.

At deep-sea fishing we admit we are not much good. We give up. Matter of fact, the giving up part is about all we know of deep-sea fishing. Just throw the line over, if you've got the strength, and throw everything else after it.

For a man getting up in years, fishing for limpets is good, although inclined to be a bit monotonous.

* * *

But for those who cannot get close to the sea, said he kindly – for those who are far from the roaring deep (said roaring caused by the bass, the drummers, the wails, and the trumpeters, besides all the other fish with internal organs), a little silver-fishing is advised.

It is best done with two players. A small piece of carpet, loaded with moth balls, is cast into the room or rooms. (Set lines may be used.)

The silverfish emerges from its den, and claws gluttonishly at the moth balls. After some hours, it reclines, sated, on the piece of carpet, and may be drawn gently to a given spot. It is here that the second player comes in. He engages the silverfish's attention with 'The Village Blacksmith' or 'The Face on the Bar-room Floor.'

* * *

The silverfish props its head on one paw, and gazes in a dazed manner at the elocutionist.

The head player then sneaks up behind it (the silverfish), grabs it by the throat, and the rest is not suitable for young readers.

We knew an expert who, without bait, caught 105 silverfish in one night, simply by reciting 'Gungha Din.'

They came and gave themselves up in dozens. There is very little more to be said about trout.

Overcoming Class Consciousness

A considerable number of Socialistic reformers advocate the cultivation of class-consciousness.

Having recently had two winning days at the ponies; and being now a capitalist, I cannot agree with them.

Noah was the first man to make the lion and the lamb sleep in the same bunk, and he, being the forerunner of Inchcape and the only man to have a menagerie and a monopoly at the same time, is entitled to some respect.

To emphasise the difference between a capitalist and a worker is to emphasise the difference between the former's income and the latter's.

Which is manifestly unfair.

Speaking as a capitalist, I would like it noted that while recognising the enormous gulf which stretches between the ordinary worker and the man of wealth who has had two successful days at the ponies, I still think that the gap should be bridged.

It would not take much bridging, and with the worker viewing life in the same way as the capitalist, it would not be long before he realised his responsibilities as a worker and ceased to be discontented.

Various highly placed personages have expressed the opinion that at least one span might be extended across the gulf if the working classes would only learn to speak with the same faultless diction as their masters.

A very good idea, and one that could be easily put into operation.

For the purposes of demonstrating the ease of it, we will examine its operation on a member, say, of the building trade.

The member of the building trade is seeking a job.

He approaches the foreman.

Removing his hat, he says: 'Pardon me, old chap; but I am seeking employment. If I can be of any assistance to you in the furtherance of your designs, I would be delighted to devote my time to your service at the usual rate.'

Sounds jolly, doesn't it?

Much better than, 'Anything doin', Joe.'

You see the idea?

Then there is the matter of dress. It would entail no hardship for a hod-carrier to come to work decently attired.

The spats and morning coat could be removed when commencing work, and the silk hat stowed away in the tucker box. It would, of course, be necessary to wear gloves while working, but then, all tools being fitted with ivory handles, the wear and tear would not be so very great.

And the social side must not be neglected. It would be a simple and courteous gesture of hospitality if the mortar-mixes were 'At Home' on Saturday afternoons to the brick-layers. The hod-carriers could give a little soiree for the plasterers, and the foreman could be made the guest of honour at the tea-boys' coming out party, and so on.

Everything would be nice and sociable, and the contractor and owner of the building would have no hesitation in inviting a select number of refined workers to meet the architect and ride out on the Ford lorry.

Courtesy need not stop at these little social events. It can and should be practised all the time.

Little thoughtful actions, like bringing flowers to the foreman, and perhaps an occasional cigar for the employer, all help to sweeten life and keep the social amenities well oiled.

Going further, concerts could be held in the lunch interval.

In the presence of good, refined music, class-consciousness is sunk, and the worker is elevated by the Muse to the level of his superiors.

And that is just what we want. Unity of outlook, the worker seeing eye to eye with the capitalist, and restraining from unreasonable requests for higher wages.

Well then, the concert!

Operatic music is good, but being sung mostly in a foreign language, it lacks the quality of sympathy that binds the classes together.

Songs such as 'We're Here Because We're Here' and 'Paddy McGinty's Goat' are, of course, impossible. What we want, then, is suitable English words set to operatic music.

I'll try and show you what I mean.

We will suppose it is lunch time. Gentlemen engaged on the job are sitting, chatting idly, discussing personalities and the latest Vice-Regal reception.

The foreman waves his baton, and the concert commences.

Something like this:

Bricklayers: 'Oh! The bally old bricks we jolly well lay.'

Hod-carriers: 'Too true, they jolly well lay them!'

Bricklayers: 'We lay them neatly – just this way' (demonstrating).

Employers, Foremen, etc.: 'And we have to jolly well pay them!'

Chorus:

Mortar-mixers: 'Oh! We mix, mix, mix!'

Bricklayers: 'And we lay, lay, lay!'

Hod-carriers: 'And we hod, hod, hod!'

Employers, etc.: 'And we pay, pay, pay!'

And so it goes on.

Now just think what an enormous difference this would make!

The refinement! The good feeling and fellowship. It would be a common occurrence for two hod-carriers to pause at the foot of a ladder and bow, murmuring at the same time, 'After you, sir!'

Isn't this much better than swearing at the foreman, and trying to drop a brick on the boss?

Of course it is.

Well, go to it. Attaboy!

I, myself, having had two good days at the ponies – I
think I have mentioned this before – but what I mean to
say is that I'd like to see you workers drag yourselves up
to my level and drop all this class-conscious stuff.

On the other hand, if you wait till after the next pony
meeting, I may be with you. In which case the gap will be
bridged by a punt!

Substantial Meals
Recipes from the Jungle

We intend to breed elephants for the market. We shall establish Elephant Clubs and hold laying competitions, awarding blue ribbons for pure-bred Buff Orpington elephants and tartan ribbons for crossbreds.

We are driven to this, partly because of the economic depression and partly because, since the Colonial Exhibition in Paris, 'The strange Oriental dishes of the Exhibition restaurants have created a taste for exotic food. Lion's flesh is in demand, and elephant's ears on toast ...'

In order to popularise the elephant with the eating public (of which there is still a large number) we publish a few recipes.

Take one elephant. Peel and soak in a lagoon overnight. Remove the ears (it is better to do this while the elephant is asleep). Fry ears to a dull black and throw on top of toast.

Serve hot.

A Good Roast

JOINT – Remove hind leg of elephant. Elephant will fall over. While in recumbent position, clean and scrape.

Take middle portion of elephant and grease well. Start bush fire. Run for life. Come back in fortnight's time. (This is good with vegetable marrows.)

SOUP – Take two elephants. Remove tusks and beat into a stiff froth. Add four gills of crushed bath-heater. Stir well and skim with long-handled shovel. Simmer for three months. Some add moth-balls (this is purely a matter of taste).

A touch of lemon is always necessary, otherwise the dish repeats. The elephant never forgets, but still one doesn't want to be reminded ALL the time. No.

EAT MORE ELEPHANTS!

A Lower Standard

One of the brightest spots in our hitherto drab life is the abolition of the gold standard in favour of a note standard.

The British Government is merely following a procedure which we have advocated and put into practice for many months past.

Some of our notes have been classics.

DEAR SIR, – Owing to the present financial depression, we find ourself unable to meet your just demands immediately. However, we are expecting shortly a legacy from a wealthy relative in Fiji, and you may rest assured ...

Then there was the other one which always worked. You simply pin the note on your door: 'BACK IN TEN MINUTES.' You then go away for eleven years, and are never heard of again.

GAS CO.

Sirs, – Your insulting message reached me this morning. Need I say that I was disgusted and annoyed? This is the fourth final notice I have had from you. Any more of this, and I shall be compelled to request you to send a man to cut off my gas supply.

This usually fixes things. Of course, there are faults in the system.

Yesterday we were presented with a note, 'I.O.U. 5/-. Signed, L. W. Lower.' So we went back to the gold standard.

The whole thing is very involved. Mean to say, come home and find on kitchen table a note, 'Waited up till 2 o'clock. Where have you been? Your dinner is in the oven.'

That sort of note is NOT negotiable.

The Perfect Husband

Love.
Five minutes ago we wrote the word. What a train of thought and happy memories ... and gas bills, and milkmen breaking the saucer with which you covered the jug.

The dear days when you held her hand, hating to let it go. These days when you are handcuffed to it, and can't go.

The perfect husband? Look us over.

A husband should be kind, gentle, and understanding. (We are speaking from experience). He should be courteous and cheerful. Economical and liberal. Stern, brave, and pusillanimous. Ready to face the tasks and cook breakfasts of the day with courage.

He should be tactful enough to ask for his tobacco money without starting a fearful row. After the row, he should sympathise with his wife, who has developed a splitting headache through shouting at him, and he should bring her aspirin tablets.

He should be a bashed-in, baggy-kneed, penniless, perambulator-pushing tea and toast-making, dog-dandling, eye-averting mutt.

Shouldn't he?

Strange how Cupid leaves his bow for his club.

LOVE!! – Mine's a pint with squash.

Ourselves Unveiled

Been looking ourself over, prior to joining the nude sun-bathing club.

We did it gradually. Removing the hat, we looked as if we were not going out. With the coat off, it would seem that we were going to do something.

The vest, collar, and tie cast aside, we resembled a weekend potterer in gardens. With the braces off, a sort of anxious look spread o'er the countenance, and a feeling of You-go-to-the-door-I-think-it's-the-landlord pervaded us.

In shirt, socks, suspenders and boots, we looked a bit ridiculous, but after tearing off the socks, boots, and suspenders we discovered a remarkable likeness in ourself to Ghandi.

With the prospect of living for rest of life on goat's milk, and seeing that the only goat we have does not give milk, we cast the shirt aside.

There we were. Our face – beautiful. Our neck raw from shaving. The shoulders bent from years of worrying about gas bills, the torso like a wrecked Zeppelin, the knees knobbly, the feet spread out, and the ankles with the funny little bones that wear your socks out.

Looking at ourself sideways, we looked like a voice crying in the wilderness. Looking at our back we got a crick in the neck.

We cannot forecast any success for the nude sunbathing club.

And another thing, imagine the political heads of our glorious State, in the nude.

Revolution! Immediately!

The cult is doomed. This, doom it may concern.

Kleptomaniacs

For being a kleptomaniac, a man got three years,
with bars, at the Quarter Sessions. The difference
between a burglar and a kleptomaniac is that one
does it for a living and the other for a hobby.

There is no fouler collection of meat (apart from tinned dingo) than a klepto. He will take anything from a dose of castor oil to a day off.

Caught red-handed in the act of bearing off a wheat silo, he will mumble that 'a strange feeling' came over him.

We feel a personal peevishness about this because of a certain packet of cigarettes which we accidentally found in a coat that was hanging on an infrequently frequented nail.

The office klepto had deviously hidden himself in the wainscote, watching with small beady eyes. We were robbed.

The unwritten law of the underworld prevented us from opening our mouth. Case of moral lockjaw.

These people have even been known to take a holiday, no mean feat mark you, even in these days of doles. Prominent politicians have come to us personally, and said that they would 'take steps to have the matter rectified.'

We have pointed out the danger of taking steps. Explained that a man living eight feet from the street level can scarcely devise a number of steps on the spur of the moment. Steps taken – liable to break neck. Great social disadvantage.

Kleptomania does not pay. What did we get on the boss's overcoat?

Chances We Missed

Any cheering to be done, who does it? We do. 'The day of vapid and inane advertising is ending. The modern advertiser who does not appeal to the customer's intellect is lost.' Get that? Lost! Bloodhounds and search parties indicated.

We get a kick out of every modern advertisement we see. After reading through an American magazine we are black and blue, and after a short period, during which we are kept under observation, are allowed to go home.

'What? A hundred and eighty years old today! My dear, you don't look a day over 170. However do you do it?'

'It's that new Creme Clammy, cherie. I just put it on between meals. And just fancy! It comes in 59 different varieties, to suit any size face!'

'Oo, la, la! I must buy a keg of it immediately!'

Now, that's the stuff to give 'em.

Take the case of that chap Wilberforce.

Wealthy, and with plenty of money. Good-looking and of noble birth, he had a luxurious steam yacht and a steam train and railway station. Yet everyone avoided him.

When he walked into the theatre the whole audience made a dive for the fire exits. He couldn't make it out.

Even his best friends wouldn't tell him.

Soon as they saw him coming they stepped on it and aimed for the nearest horizon. But at last one of his enemies told him – by telegram. You guessed it – he had halitosis. Ninety per cent of our divorce cases are due solely to this ravaging disease.

That makes you sit up, doesn't it?

Then there was that other fellow.

He thought: 'Holy Mike! Another second of this and I'm asphyxiated!' But, just to be polite, he said: 'you stick there. I'm going to throw myself under a tram.'

That ought to be enough to make any self- respecting girl go and wash herself all over with Lifer's Soap.

Take our own case. We received a letter saying, 'Are you an unemployed labourer? WHY NOT BECOME AN UNEMPLOYED ARCHITECT?' We could have been anything; electrical engineer, lift-driver, deep-sea diver; all by signing the dotted line and sending no money.

We became an architect in three weeks. Our wife, who read all the instructions, became an architect too. If young Wally had been old enough to read he'd have been an architect.

We used to practise on each other. The wife would fall through the front door and say: 'I got that there raise, Mabel! That brings me up to four hundred dollars per, an' nex' week they're going to make me managing director!'

And I'd say: 'And it's all due to the Interchangeable Correspondence School! Now we'll be able to get that red and yeller blanket we've always wanted.'

When we sit down and strap ourself into a chair and think of how on earth we got on before there were any advertisements, when we didn't have pyorrhoea or halitosis, or unsightly hairs, skin blemishes, no ambition, couldn't play music on a saw, couldn't hold board meetings spellbound and were never offered the opportunity to earn 1000 dollars a week giving away packets of giant beans ... well, it makes us feel sorry for us, when we look back on ourself.

A Tip for the Treasurer
Making Money with Bicycles

'I started out to ride around the world on a bicycle in 1908. I left Melbourne with a penny in my pocket, and after working my way across Africa, England, and America, I arrived back in Melbourne in 1914 with 4/6.' Thus Mr H. A. Tipper has just come to town with an assortment of bicycles.

With all due respect to Mr Tipper, we should like to relate how we started out with fourpence on four bicycles, went four times round the world backwards, and came back 18/- in debt.

Then there was the time we had eightpence and started off on eight bicycles – but we will not weary you (Oh, NO!)

What we don't know about bicycles is known only to the bicycle itself. We have ridden bicycles down till the spokes were mere stubs and the handle-bars were dragging on the ground.

We started on a cyclone (from 'cycl,' meaning cycle, and 'one,' meaning one – a one-wheeled bicycle). Then we invented the gravity-bike. This could be ridden downhill only.

However, it was not until we got to the motorcycle

stage that we really prospered. At first they were fairly popular, breaking down in fairly populous places, and thus enabling the rider to display his vocabulary to the admiring populace.

Later we added side-cars, complete with cycles, which broke down in the bush somewhere about Penrith.

Our real triumph was the bicycle wheel which spoke for itself.

Of course we innovated (a good word) the Spring seats. They were not much good in the Winter.

But we are afraid that in our enthusiasm we have wandered a little from the point.

Our suggestion is that, following the lines of Mr Tipper, the Treasurer start out with 7/6 on 120 bicycles and go 3000 times around the world and come back with sufficient to pay the national debt.

And even if he never came back ... ?

TUSH! What's a few bicycles?

Banking
How She Works

Being an Heroic Attempt at an Explanation

A rudimentary knowledge of banking and banks does not necessarily imply the possession of a bank balance. One might as well demand that anti-vivisectionists be partly vivisected so that they may back their antipathy with personal and acute experience.

My actual experience in the matter of banking is such that if all the notes I had banked were placed end to end they would reach ...

What's the lineal measure for atom?

While in my callow youth, and spurred on by the fierce pangs of love, I banked ten shillings. Two days later I reluctantly withdrew it, and my account was closed forever. If Sunday had not intervened I might have had it out earlier.

This rambling explanation is intended, not so much as an apology, as a proof that one needn't have money in the bank to have an interest in banks. All right then.

Small metal tokens of some intrinsic value and coloured strips of paper – which, in the middle of the Sahara desert, could only be prized in so far as their artistic merit appealed – are money.

Money is a means of facilitating exchange.

That is to say, the possession of a pound-note saves you the trouble of carrying five hundredweight of home-grown potatoes down to Anthony Horderns' when you wish to buy a pair of boots.

Likewise, the institution of the monetary system prevents the boss from paying you in alarm clocks.

The first man to become wealthy accumulated his hoard very slowly. Finding himself with a surplus of pumpkins, he swapped a few of them with neighbors in adjoining caves, for stone clubs, bear-skins, and whatnot.

Nature pursued its relentless course and foisted more pumpkins on to him. By degrees he accumulated an enormous stock of bear skins, etcetera, as well as pumpkins.

Came a drought or an earthquake. We forget now which it was. The bears died off in hundreds. For want of a feed of pumpkin the stone club maker was too weak to make stone clubs.

(This is where we deviate a little from historical accuracy, for the sake of the analogy.)

The drought or the earthquake eased off, and Nature took up her burden of making bears.

But things were very bad.

One day a man came to the cave of the pumpkin millionaire.

'Look here,' he said, in his simple, straight-forward way. 'I've got an idea for growing woad plants. There'll be a big demand for woad presently, and it's a great proposition.'

'Well?' queried the wealthy one languidly. 'What about it?'

'I'm broke,' answered the other. 'Will you finance me?'

'What security have you?'

'Well, I've an extensive cave, fur-lined throughout, in a good defensive position, free from pterodactyls; also four wives, two being practically new and the other two so thoroughly domesticated that they grovel every time I raise my club. I should say the lot was worth about 100 stone clubs or 300 pumpkins at the present rate of exchange.'

'H'm! How much do you want?'

'Eighty clubs should be sufficient to put my woad plantation on a working basis.'

They went into details. At last the pumpkinaire, after convincing himself that there was a good demand for woad, that the intending borrower was a hard worker, and that he knew all about woad, decided to finance him. He accordingly financed him with fifty clubs, taking the hundred club's worth of cave and wives as a security.

At the end of the year the borrower was to return sixty clubs for the fifty lent.

The woad plantation got under way, and that was that.

Men in adjoining caves heard of the enterprising woad planter's success, and came in droves to the cave of the pumpkinaire. If he fancied their projects and liked their security, he financed them.

Now, this is where the funny part comes in. Everybody knew that the pumpkinaire was wealthy, and one day a man came to borrow thirty bear skins, as he was converting his cave into flats. And the pumpkinaire didn't have a skin in the place.

This is what he did.

He said: 'Take this smooth stone with the funny mark on it to the fellow over the river. Tell him to give you thirty bear skins, and when he returns that stone to me I'll pay him.'

The fellow did as he was told.

Said the man over the river: 'It's a bit unusual, but I know the pumpkinaire. He is a man of wealth. He always pays up. This stone is worth thirty bear skins any old day in the week.'

It worked, you see, and the pumpkinaire thought deeply on the matter. He began to see that it was only a matter of a big reputation, a few stones, and faith on the part of the stoneholders.

The stone came back; the pumpkinaire paid up, and lent the stone out again. It circulated. People began to know that it was worth thirty bear skins.

The pumpkinaire got more stones, and marked them with his private mark. The day came when he had 3000 pumpkins' worth of stones in circulation and only 500 pumpkins. It made no difference. People believed in him.

Behold, the first bank.

Now, let us consider. If in his eagerness to grab, the banker made 1000 stones when the total value of all the goods in the community was only 500 stones, he inflated the currency. The stone that was supposed to be worth 30 bear skins would only be worth 15 bear skins.

The money wealth of the community would be 1000 stones.

The real wealth would be 500 stones' worth of goods and 500 stones' worth of faith (or belief in the banker's ability to pay).

Possessed of only 500 stones' worth of real wealth, the community has to pay back to the banker 1000 stones, plus interest. (Be patient. It's dreadfully difficult to keep from getting tangled up.)

Now you can see that with its measly 500 stones the community will have to work like mad, twice as hard as they ought, to pay back the banker's thousand.

You can see that people are going to economise in all directions. You can see how the slaves will be put on short rations. You can see the unemployment coming.

You can see why, when we borrow abroad, pledging the horny hands of Australia as security, we must pay back in gold or privileges.

We must pay back in something tangible – not faith-notes.

You can see that 5,000,000 American dollars is – or is supposed to be – 5,000,000 dollars' worth of American goods. We may do what we like with the money, buy English goods if we like, but sooner or later, by the simple process of exchange, that money must go back to America. And in America that five million represents five millions' worth of goods.

We don't borrow money; we borrow goods.

Wiping the sweat off our eye-shade we pause for breath, and admit that we have bitten off more than we can chew.

Banking is a big subject, and stretches as far beyond the scope of this article as a verbatim report of the proceedings at the Tower of Babel.

Like trying to put your pet whale in a glass bowl to fraternise with the gold-fish.

But stop cheering. We haven't finished yet. Sorry.

We would just like to point out the possibilities, the ramifications and the power of banks and bankers.

We would like to point out that the business of banking is something that affects you - even if you haven't got a 'crab' to your name.

You can see that the big bankers can promote industry, or put the brakes on it simply by giving or withholding loans.

You can see that they are the Master Minds behind the capitalist.

You can see that they hold us in the hollow of their hands.

Do you see the necessity for Government control of banking?

Currency Based on Experience

We have a PLAN. Before we go any further, it would be best, perhaps, to give a rough explanation of our monetary situation, particularly where it touches our fiscal fiduciaries.

No. Maybe we hadn't better ...

Our Plan is really the introduction of a practical currency based on the experience of a lifetime.

We propose to have printed, notes of various denominations and sizes.

The nineteen and elevenpence three farthings note will be about 12 inches square and suitable for use at millinery sales.

The 37/6, or Boarding House note will be a little larger, so that the boarder, having paid the landlady with it, the landlady may then wrap the boarder's lunch in it.

From there we go to the £5, £10, and £20 issues, which will be of correspondingly larger size, enabling one to wrap up larger parcels.

We have another bright idea for keyhole-shaped coins. These would be especially useful after hours. The trouble would be to get keyhole-shaped bottles. We'd probably bring in an Enlarged Keyholes (Amendment) Act.

All this is detail.

Broadly, the Lower Plan consists in printing some tens of millions of five pound notes and distributing two to each of the population. Of course, they would be worth only about 5/- each, but that would be 10/-, anyhow; and who is in need of ten shillings?

STAND BACK! The Plan hasn't started yet.

But is it any good! Mais, oui!

Nothing Like Love

Love is an abstract thing used by soft people as something to take their minds off their work. If it were a concrete thing it would be too hard for most of us. You may cement friendships, but concrete love is mortar-fying.

Some say love is a disease, but it's less of a disease than a complaint. No woman incapable of complaining ever gets married.

Ask any married man.

Love is a thing that gnaws into your bosom and then recommends a good brand of ointment, and will bandage you up so that you get worse.

The term, 'He fell in love,' is significant. He fell in – Love.

Men who fall deeply in love go off their meals. After they get married they go off for their meals. Love is universal. It is just the same in Darlinghurst as it is in Oodnadatta, only in Darlinghurst it happens at shorter intervals.

Love-sick is a term generally applied to those in love. It shouldn't be.

Love makes the world go round. That's why it is flattened at both ends.

Love is to man a thing apart (and better that way), 'tis woman's whole existence (especially where the alimony is concerned).

There is nothing like love.

As for bargain sales – well, a husband is woman's most precious bargain.

£ove ! £ove! £ove.

How Can You Tell If You Are Silly?

We are getting a bit nervous about this agitation to revise the lunacy laws. So far, we are still at large, along with a lot of other people, but you never know.

A man who makes laws compelling you to vote yourself into misery, or be fined £2, is capable of anything.

It is so hard to tell when a man has the bats. The questioning method is not much good.

This sort of thing:

'Is your father sane?'

'Sayin' what?'

'I mean, is there any insanity in your family?'

'Our family has always been sanitary.'

'Was your great-grandmother a Moron?'

'No. She was a Presbyterian.' ... that sort of thing gets you nowhere.

Actions count more than words. Only yesterday we met a friend who knew us well, and we asked him for a loan of a tenner.

He said, 'Certainly!' and gave it to us. We blanched with fear, and grasping the note, hurried away.

We're going to avoid that man for the future.

The surest way to discover a lunatic is to place before him his income tax assessment, his gas bill, rent bill, electric light bill, etcetera.

If he leaps up and sings, 'Happy Days Are Here Again!' and walks to the rathouse under his own power – he's sane.

If he sits down, places his forehead in his hand, and says, 'Lor, I dunno what I'm going to do about this,' and starts searching his pockets, he's raving mad, and should be given the full rights of a citizen of our glorious Commonwealth.

Women Gamblers Shouldn't

As the only man who ever threw an egg sandwich on the wheel at Monte Carlo and stopped the works, we are deeply interested in the new rule of the International Sporting Club, which bars women gamblers.

The last time we were on the Riviera four women suicided. Whether it was because they lost heavily, or because of our tragic beauty, we are too modest to say, but the fact remains, if they hadn't been gambling they wouldn't have seen us, and probably would have been alive today, though unthrilled. Women should not gamble.

They should not gamble, because when they lose, their husbands have nothing to take to the races on Saturday.

They should remember, when tempted to have a few bob on something at the S.P. joint, that every eightpence lost is a pound of sausages gone west.

This careless 'There goes the gas money' attitude which many women adopt is distinctly ruinous.

The landlord may be beaten by a short head for the rent, but very few landlords are sporting enough to accept the sad news with a smile and a 'Never mind. Try again next week.'

Women haven't the stamina for gambling. Very few can conceal that goose flesh feeling brought on by four aces, they cannot walk long distances from remote places like Canterbury, Rosehill, and Warwick Farm, and most of them can't shuffle for nuts.

And besides, they get home too late to get the tea ready and a man can't live on tinned salmon ALL the time.

Anyhow, they don't need to gamble. They get the cash ultimately, just the same.

A man wins a few quid, comes home, has it confiscated, and is given 1/6 to buy tobacco with. And then he says he's had a winning day!

Ha! Ha! Ha! It makes me laugh sardonically!

Rules for Husbands

A big mistake has been made by Albert Ross, of Jersey City, U.S.A.

His bride drew up 47 rules for their mutual guidance, which rules included everything from attending church to the division of salary.

Until he signed, his wife refused to kiss him. Albert refused to sign, and the marriage was annulled.

We signed. Anyone puts anything up to us and says, 'Sign this!' we always sign it. It's most exciting. We never know whether we are going to have a time-payment gramophone delivered next day or a block of land, or be arrested.

What we signed was something about, 'You will not walk on the carpet. You will not splash any water on the bathroom floor when taking a shower. You will refrain from sitting on the edge of the bed after it has been made.

'You will not touch the decanter, which is for the visitors. You will not burn holes in the lounge; you will not dirty my clean ash-trays; you will always wipe your muddy boots before you come in.

'You will not leave any doors open, or go about the place switching lights on and not switching them off.

'No throwing of clothes all over the floor when getting undressed, no taking the matches from the kitchen, no being nasty to my mother; you will not encourage my brother to drink, and you will not be more than three-quarters of a minute late for dinner.'

And believe us, we have had more fun breaking those rules than anything else you could think of. Only trouble is, we are running short of rules.

An Admission of Ancestry
How one Becomes Reincarnated

The statements of Mrs Annie Besant and Bishop Leadbeater, that they remember every one of their lives and reincarnations right back to the time when they were slimy, lizard-like creatures, encourages us to make a few admissions of our own.

We were once a sponge cake.

We remember as if it was yesterday, lying there in that prehistoric refreshment room for months and months and months; it might have been years.

Then came our first reincarnation. We were taken down, dusted, and put in among the rock cakes. We forget exactly how long after that we were donated to the soup kitchen.

From then on, our reincarnations were rapid. From a rock cake we became an attack of indigestion, after which we were a jelly-fish, a politician, a vulture, and a rhinoceros.

Improving all the time you'll notice.

It was just when we had finished being a rhinoceros that complications set in. Fate seemed undecided whether it would make us a hip-bath or a sewing machine.

We finished up as a glugflobber, a rather curious

animal which lives solely on bicycle-pumps and the black portions of draught boards. Its only means of propulsion is to make a loud noise behind its own back, thus frightening itself into taking a leap forward.

Need we tell you of the various stages we passed through? Of when we were a freedlupper, wheeling our ego in front of us and spearing complexes with our sharp-pointed inhibitions? No. We needn't.

But there is one thing we should like to explain. It is about the time when we were Lord Nelson. We did NOT put the telescope to our blind eye and say, 'I see no signals.'

We put the telescope to our good eye and said, 'I see no (HIC!) shignals.' After this we got properly shot, and as we fell to the deck Hardy bent over us and we said, 'Hiccups, Hardy.'

And Hardy, misunderstanding, kissed us.

We are now on our present plane. It is only a matter of time when we shall reach the pinnacle toward which civilisation has been gradually forging all these countless ages.

We shall become one of the unemployed.

And, on that plane, there is nothing but eternal rest.

A Waggish Tail

A strong argument for Manx dogs has been introduced by the manager of the King Edward Dogs' Home, who was paid £19/5/- for the tails of 154 stray dogs at 2/6 a tail.

It would pay us and our father-in-law to keep a lot of dogs and buy cigarettes with them, getting 1/6 change; which would be spent on more dogs; thus making us a millionaire and forcing us to drag ourself enthusiastically off the labor market.

It might even be possible, after prolonged research, to invent a dog which grew one tail after another, indefinitely.

A man with a herd of dogs could put the Income Tax Department to a lot of well-earned trouble.

On the other hand, a man with one dog would probably, in these times, say in a choked voice: 'Here, Boy! Commorn! Commorn!'

He would look the dog in the eye, sorrowfully. Steeling himself, he would say, 'You may be a dog to me, but you're only a half-crown in the bank's refrigerator.'

It has its sad moments, but it also has its economic possibilities. Such as, 'Excuse me, but have you change of a bull terrier?'

'Sorry, but all I have is an Airedale pup and two

Chow Chows.'

You then walk away disappointed, as usual. Which is the basis of all economics.

Talking of Worms

A man, whose name we will not mention, on account of the vile crime which he did and which we do not wish to be slung up in front of his countless ancestors, yet unborn, and the whole neighbourhood taking a day off to go and point the finger of scorn, the sturdier members getting out their shovels and heaping ignominy on him – he was fined £2 with 8s. costs at Court.

He was caught red-handed, digging worms at Sans Souci, thus annoying the oyster-leasers, and was charged with having 'unlawfully taken worms' and with 'unlawfully having caught worms on a closed area.'

And to think that that man was once an innocent little babe, lounging at his mother's knee!

As for us, we can say with a certain amount of pride that we have never taken worms. We have taken everything else, from pills to mustard baths and aspirins, but so far we haven't shown any serious and determined hankering for worms.

But, of course, we know a good deal about them. There are two kinds of worms. Long worms and short worms.

The long worms can be easily distinguished from the short worms; the head of the short worm being invariably closer to the tail than in the case of the long worm.

It has long puzzled scientists how the worm finds a hole to fit it.

Nature in its awful wisdom has provided holes of various sizes all over our vast and glorious continent. All the worm has to do is to tramp about and find a hole that fits.

We knew of one worm with goitre that walked from Coogee to Parramatta before it found a suitable home. Even then it was only a semi-detached hole, being next to a quarry.

The grub is very close to the worm and could quite easily be taken for a worm by anyone who has never seen a worm. The only difference between the two is that the one has more legs, and more hair on its chest than the other. The grub is also better upholstered.

Aborigines regard grubs as a delicacy and will chase them for miles, hurling boomerangs at them.

Other kinds are found underneath logs – although how the devil those little chaps balance those great logs has got us beat.

We cannot speak with any authority on the subject, but we presume that the grub lies on its back and then pulls the log over itself.

The centipede is really an armor-plated worm, equipped with a knife and fork at one end. It has a lot of legs, an incalculable number, and how it keeps in step? ... We won't bother about it. Once you start thinking about things like that, you go mad and run around in circles barking like a dog.

Wool and What It All Means

Today Wool Week begins, but just because you're wearing a woollen singlet you needn't look sheepish.

Wool is our greatest product next to mutton. Woolgrowing is the laziest occupation in the world, as the sheep does all the growing part and the owner merely goes out at intervals and tears the wool off the sheep.

The primitive method of hand-plucking has long been out of date, but as yet no one has invented a fleece for sheep on the hook and eye principle. Buttons along the back of the sheep are obviously impracticable. A man can't go chasing sheep about the place every time they lose a button.

For a long time we have been advocating the putting of red stripes on each end of sheep intended for making blankets.

This would save putting them on later. The stripes on blankets are necessary, of course, so people will be able to tell the top and bottom ends of the bed, and will not retire crossways.

Sheep frequently get tick, in which they are far superior to us, we being unable to get it anywhere. They also get burrs (some of the sheep in Scotland are barely understandable) and dirt in the fleece.

This need not worry those intending to buy a woollen singlet, as most of these foreign bodies are taken out of the singlet when it is made, and what few burrs are left occasion very little discomfort unless they happen to be under the armpits.

Topweight Snail's Great Run

A wanderer in the wilds of Parramatta has returned with the report that a number of the unemployed residents of the district were observed crowding around five snails, which were crawling towards a cabbage leaf.

The betting was described as 'frantic.'

If it is to be revived, we should like to see this old sport put on a proper footing. Dirty tactics, like putting lime on the track just near the home turn, and ringing-in periwinkles, should not be tolerated.

A glaring instance of roguery will be remembered by old timers when the old Central Snailway was in existence.

In a handicap event, Slobber, a very poor performer who had been brought down from the country, was the medium of some heavy plunges, and romped home in front of a classy field.

The stewards found at the inquiry that Slobber's shell had been shaved down, and the owner, trainer and snail were disqualified for life.

The Carbine of all snails was Greasy, who humped his shell, and half an ounce of chewing gum, over a fifty-yard course and finished in the remarkable time of 2 days

21 hours dead.

He was never any good after this supreme effort.

A badly trained snail is a cow to play up at the barrier, and keeping this in mind, it would be well for owners to have their snails trained from the time they are slugs.

Matter of Chance

Lay them back in the moth-balls and lavender; the 12 horseshoes we wore yesterday because it was Friday, the 13th.

The four-leafed clover is withered and you can put away your ladders. You'll have to decide for yourself about the snakes.

We wore our sacred gallstone yesterday and it did us no good. Most unlucky. Had a ticket in the 16th State Lottery and didn't win first prize.

This is a remarkable coincidence, because we didn't win first prize with our last ticket. There must be some mystic significance in that.

Black cats are unlucky. We know this for a fact, because we kicked one yesterday afternoon when we found it eating our chop.

Thank heavens we hung on to our lucky sixpence. The tram conductor bit it and then handed back what he couldn't digest and said, 'Crook.'

We had to get out and walk, and it probably saved our life up till now, because we don't get enough exercise and might die of fatty degeneration at any minute.

We have decided that luck is all a matter of chance.

New Opera

Spurred on by the successful debut of the first Jewish opera in Sydney, the Scottish community is working hard to arrange a Scotch opera.

There will be an orchestra of 50 bagpipes and 18 drums. Twelve big drums and six bigger drums.

Admission tickets may be purchased on the lay-by or at the door.

The McGagget clan has expressed its willingness to collect at the box office, and suitable first aid facilities have been arranged for the benefit of those people who try to get in free. Promissory notes will not be accepted.

The story of the opera is woven round a feud between two old clans as to the possession of a bent thruppence which was found on the border of the two estates.

The love motif would bring tears to the eyes of a deaf Chinese pugilist. The chieftain's daughter, who is sent to poison the rival chieftain's son's haggis, falls in love with the man she is sent to destroy, because he has gold fillings in his teeth.

Sung by Maggie Macraggers, 'Oh, Smile at Me again' is touching enough to make an eiderdown mattress quack.

When the 50 bagpipes and the 18 drums join in the last tender passages, it would be scarcely possible to hear a pin drop, even if any one of the audience was careless enough to drop it.

The climax is reached when the victorious chieftain has to hold the disputed thruppence in his hand and sing, 'Bent But Not Broke.'

In Glasgow, the stage was mobbed while this scene was taking place. It is not known who got the thruppence.

In Darkest Africa!

Soon, by means of wireless and television, a man may sit at home in Sydney and see and hear the explorer in the jungles of Darkest Africa, says a weekly paper.

Which is pretty crook. You can't get a bit of privacy now, even in the jungle. It was different when we were in Darkest Africa.

We were in the darkest part of Darkest Africa where even the natives are dark and you can't see your hand before your face. Many's the time we've been trudging along and run into our hand, inflicting severe bruises. We shall never forget the time when we camped on the M'Bongopongo. Our head boy came dashing to our tent, crying, 'M'pah Moogow!' (We're known as M'pah Moogow by the natives, the name meaning 'GREAT WHITE MASSA WHO STRANGLES PANTHERS WITH ONE HAND WHILE LIGHTING HIS PIPE.') It seems that a large tiger was eating the cook. Hastily loading our rifle, which was never out of our hands, we ran to the spot.

The tiger glanced up and bounded towards us, yelping furiously.

We fired our first barrel, but still he came on. The second failed to stop him, so picking up the first barrel, we rolled it towards him. He tripped over it, and while he was down we brained him with the other barrel.

Unfortunately, the bung came out and we lost a lot of valuable stuff. It's things like that that make an explorer's life so hazardous.

He was a fair specimen of a tiger, measuring 22 feet from nose to tail. The largest we ever shot was one which measured eight miles from nose to tail. We blew his tail off, and we estimate that he covered about eight miles before pulling up.

We were the only man in Darkest Africa to play quoits on a rhinoceros, putting up a break of twenty-five before he charged us and was felled with a straight left, fair between the eyes.

We were the only man to penetrate into the gorilla country alone and walk out alive. So far as we know, in no single instance has anyone walked out dead.

But not always were we so lucky.

One day, sitting before our G'blonko, or tent, we thought we would amuse the natives, so we drew out our Zangle-Zangle, or Saxophone. They laughed when we sat down to play, but when we had blown a few notes they screamed loudly and beat it into the jungle. And all because we had filled in a coupon and learned in seven days by the NOMUSIC SYSTEM.

Left alone, except for a few tigers and alligators, we realised that the position was serious and decided to make for the coast. We shudder now when we think of that dreadful journey. Tramping through the rotted vegetation in the steaming jungle, jaguars dropping down our neck from trees above, sleeping rolled up in a boa constrictor to keep warm in the chilly nights. Living on wild berries (Oh, we haven't finished yet), leaves, roots, and such zebras as we managed to run down. And what nutriment is there in a zebra when it's run-down.

At last we reached the coast (yes, we are just as grateful as you are), and gradually working our way down, arrived at Woy Woy. We were put to bed with delirium tremens, and emerged eight weeks later, the shadow of our former self. As a matter of fact, on dull days we were not visible to the naked eye. We are a bit better now, but every now and then, a touch of the old complaint comes back to us to remind us of those days in Zamboanga, M'Bongopongo, Zambozle, and other places too numerous to mention.

And the old Colonel gazed reflectively into the fire ...

How To Find Out If Spiders Are Poisonous

We learnt at a lecture on spiders at the Museum last night that there are 1200 varieties of spider in Australia, but only three of them are known to be poisonous.

We are not in a position to affirm or deny this, as we do not care to be bitten by 1200 spiders just to find whether there is a fourth venomous one.

A spider usually has four pairs of eyes, and so far as we could gather, not one solitary eyebrow.

While stressing the serious effects of a poisonous spider-bite, the lecturer explained that a well-known doctor had assured him that the aboriginal method of scarifying the bitten part, and then having relays of blacks to suck out the poison still remained the best method of treatment.

It therefore will be seen that by far the safest method of getting about in a garden or other spiderous place is to be followed by relays of blacks. This, however, in a small garden may be impracticable.

Singular intelligence is displayed by the spider in that it is unable to take nourishment except in the form of liquid. This probably accounts for their ferocity when pushed or sniggered at.

Apart from a few trifling things about legs and webs etcetera, this was about all the lecturer knew about spiders.

Untrue Facts About Snakes

Healthy black snakes of 4 feet 6 inches or over will be paid for by the Taronga Park Trustees. This, according to the 'Sun,' is 'a chance for our unemployed.'

It seems to us also that there will be fewer unemployed after they have finished with the snakes.

Or, we may yet hear whisperings in the lounge of the Hotel Australia, 'Yes, they say he made his money entirely out of snakes.'

We consulted Chambers' encyclopaedia and learned that a snake has no legs, but travels by means of its scales. Which is tough on the Tramway Department.

The adder is sum snake. It has no eyelids, but sees out of its snaked eye.

It may interest the unemployed to learn that the female snake is larger than the male, and the male cannot be stretched except in cases where it gets away. Then you can say anything.

The viper is a Jewish snake closely allied to the pen-viper, and the dish-viper. It sheds its skin twice a year, but no one can find the shed.

The black snake is black, and may easily be told, although it is partially deaf. In catching the black snake, grasp it firmly behind the back of the ears, and ahead of the squirm. Should it bite, on no account bite it back, as snakes are poisonous.

It is far better, if bitten, to rub the snake with permanganate of potash, at the same time tying a ligature between the snake and the bitten portion. This method only fails on occasions.

Now a parting world. Measure the snake carefully before catching it. If it is less than 4 feet 6 inches long, don't waste your time.

Small snakes may be charmed with a tin whistle. Black snakes need a jazz band.

Remember your geometry. A straight line is the shortest distance between a snake and some other place.

Anzac Night in the Gardens

Lost in the wilds of the Botanic Gardens! Heavens, shall we ever forget it! The last human face we saw was that of Matthew Flinders, the great explorer.

We got in with a few Anzacs last night, and we forget how we got into the Gardens, but believe us, it's terrible. Instructive, but terrible.

Nothing to drink but goldfish.

Bottle-trees dotted about the place, and we had no opener. Naked men and women standing on square white-washed rocks. All dumb!

We wandered up to a signboard, thinking to read, 'Ten miles to...,' and saw there, 'Please do not walk on the grass borders.'

Starving, practically, we climbed a coconut tree for food and found it was a date tree without any dates on it.

We came to a tree marked 'Dysoxolum.' We thought – we KNEW – how sox were dyed – but what shall it profit a man if he lose himself in the Gardens?

We came to where the tortoise slept, and knocked on his shell. Like all the rest of our friends, he was in, but he didn't answer.

Dawn found us clawing at the front of the Herbarium, shrieking hysterically for just a little thyme.

The keeper who found us said that everything was all

right and this was the way out. We don't know what became of the others.

Probably their bodies will be found in the band-stand and identified by their pawn tickets.

The Anzacs certainly were, and still are, a tough crowd.

We will never go into the Gardens again without wearing all our medals and two identification discs.

It's always best to carry a spare on Anzac night.

Police say Ha! Ha!

'Police laughed yesterday at the suggestion that a clash between rival gangs was responsible for a wild shooting episode on Saturday night in Surry Hills. Inquiries showed that the incident was a display of bravado on the part of half a dozen hoodlums. One man, who had been hit with a bottle, was taken to Sydney Hospital.' – News item.

. .

We can see it. Struck on the head by a bottle, the victim giggling himself into a state of unconsciousness. Laughing heartily, the police placed him in the ambulance. The doctor chuckled softly as he stitched up the wound. He said it was the best he'd seen yet, and had the patient heard the one about the Scotsman, the Irishman, and the Jew?

Out of pure bravado, the victim coughed blood, and then swooned.

The police then laughed heartily again, patting the victim on the back, and telling him he was a fair devil.

Outside the hospital seven shots were fired at the policemen, who, having a sense of humor, grinned broadly.

He then expired on the pavement.

Shrieking with merriment, the other policemen

walked across the road and arrested one of the gunmen for a joke.

The gunman was charged next day with 'showing off' and playing practical jokes.

'It's as good as a circus,' remarked the judge. (Laughter).

Beckonings of Fame

Marathon swimming is not to be decried by the unthinking masses. Life is strange, and who knows the moment he may be called upon to swim for 75 hours 35 min. 11 sec.?

Nobody.

We dare say to any one of you that asked NOW at what moment you would be called upon to remain in water for 75 hours 35 min. 11 sec., you could not answer us.

We have, however, a gnawing sorrow. We were pointed out in a crowd.

The pointer said: 'See him? He once stayed in the water for 75 hours (etc.).'

And the pointee said: 'Why?'

Since then we have been a broken man.

Mrs Katerina Nehua insists that for her next marathon swim she must have warm water.

Sympathy leaks out of our every pore. We have been a marathoner for some time. We hold the world's record for loofah-whanging.

We once managed to stand a leaking shower drip on us for half an hour while lying in a warm bath. This is unofficial, as there was no timekeeper present.

In other branches of bath sports we were less fortunate. In the world's soap-finding contest we slipped on the soap and luckily landed on our sponge. This disqualified us. The next year we were disqualified again.

It was said of us that we took off from the wash-basin and went in off the bath-heater, contrary to regulations. After considerable argument it was ruled that the bath-heater was not a part of the bath within the meaning of the Act.

It was then that we took to marathon swimming. We stayed in the water for 75 hours 3 min., being fed with a shotgun in the meantime.

We have decided, in the light of that experience, that before we swim again the water must be thicker and properly flattened out.

Golf

We're sick of golf. We've never played; but still, that doesn't prevent us from being sick.

Sent to the Moore Park links yesterday morning to watch Jimmy Pike and partner play fellow jockey Cook and friend.

They were a bit late, so we went away. Very lucky escape it was.

Do you know that it's nearly two miles around that course, and mostly uphill? And that is as the crow flies, mark you. And we make bold to assert that even a crow would kick at all that uphill stuff.

There's not a solitary tram on the course. If you want to go from one hole to another, you've got to walk. You can't go wrong in believing us when we tell you that we were astonished.

We saw a few golfers wandering about the place while we were there. They wear their trousers tucked into their socks. We suppose this is on account of the grasshoppers. They carry a bag of tools with them for the purpose of hitting a ball into small holes which are bored in the ground by artificial means.

When two are playing together they have a ball each in order to prevent quarrelling.

The method of hitting the ball is simple. One selects,

haphazard, one of the bats from the container. The next move is to arrange the legs fairly wide apart, so that there is no possibility of falling over. The blunt instrument is then lifted above the head and the ball is struck. This counts one. Not once did we notice a player count it two. Which shows that these people are at least honest and have some sort of rough code of ethics.

Having struck the ball, the golfer then walks after it. Having caught up to it, he then strikes it again. This goes on indefinitely.

We can see now that polo was invented by a golfer who woke up to himself.

We must reluctantly admit that we cannot recommend the game of golf.

It has but one redeeming feature. We understand that when any player puts his ball into a hole in one swipe, or 'holes out in one,' as they quaintly put it, everybody immediately gets drunk.

Well, of course, that's something.

Xmas Food Annoys Us

Every time we hear a rooster crow, we feel sick. Ever since Xmas Day.

We know you don't want to hear anything about Xmas Day, but some well-meaning friends have invited us to a New Year's eve dinner. It threatens to be something like Xmas dinner, and we're not going.

It's about time somebody with a certain amount of influence, like us, said something about this dinner business.

We've gone to an enormous lot of trouble to get Monsieur Patrick O'Reilly, head chef at the Hole in the Wall, to compile an ideal menu for NEXT year.

'Ze – what you say? – ze cocktail, 'e should come first. For zis eet is best one pint of cold beer. Eef eet is to be a beeg dinner, three pints of cold beer,' said M. O'Reilly.

The chef's suggested menu is:—

PRAWNS WITH WHISKERS

Soup (off).

BEER.

'Arf and 'arf.

BEER.

'Curried Tongue' avec spuds.

BEER.

'Set of Smalls' avec floor varnish or sauce.

'Single' aux peas.

MORE BEER.

Prawns avec whiskers.

ALE.

'Ze menu is veree sniftaire and bonzaire,' said the chef. 'Eet is so much bettaire to eat 'im standing up. One can zen chase ze little pea when 'e pop off ze knife, wizout knocking ze chair ovair.'

A very sensible idea, too.

More Murders Solved

WELL! Well! If it's not the gentle reader!

Where you bin since last week? Old folk well? That's fine.

Now, just a minute ... QWERT YUIOP! ASDFGHJKL? ZXCVBNM£.

All set. The typewriter has been a bit off color lately.

DETECTIVE STORY. The effect is better if you put the lights out and read it in the dark.

We were seated at our desk one morning in June, dolefully playing on our mouth organ, when in rushed Dr Watson in a great flurry.

'What's on, Watson?' we drawled.

'Heard you the first time,' he replied, 'A vile crime has been committed at the Granaries, Lady Goober's town house.'

Snatching up our theodolite and other odds and ends which were lying about the study we dashed out into the night. Need we tell you about that wild drive in the teeth of a raging gale that fateful night? No?

Well, that saves a lot of trouble.

'This is a very bad case,' said Inspector Wills, as he greeted us at the door.

'Whatever you say is in strict confidence, of course,' we replied in an abstracted manner.

'Well then,' said the Inspector, 'I think your friend

Watson is a big mug. This is the room.'

There on the floor lay nine bodies.

(Why stint yourself? Make it ten.)

There on the floor lay eleven bodies. (Satisfied?) Each with a dagger through its heart.

'Any footprints?' we asked.

'The murderer wore boots, so as not to leave any footprints,' said the Inspector. 'We found the grindstone he used for sharpening the daggers in the bathroom.'

'Finger prints?'

'We found the file the miscreant used to file his fingers off with,' said the Inspector. 'I must admit that I am baffled.'

We glanced slowly around the room.

'The murderer had a ginger moustache,' we said.

'However did you guess!' gasped the Inspector.

'He was also the proprietor of a fruit barrow,' we continued, ignoring him. 'You will notice that only eleven were bumped off. Any ordinary man would have made it the even dozen.'

'Is there anything missing from the house?'

'Only the murderer,' replied the Inspector.

We thought this over. It complicated matters. We had never yet failed to elucidate a mystery. Our professional reputation was at stake.

The inspector watched us with growing contempt.

'We have it!' we said at last, pausing in our stride. 'Never yet have we been beaten.'

They gasped.

'It was me,' we said simply.

'Well I'll be ...' said the Inspector, and a look of hideous jealousy came into his eyes.

'You don't get away with that sort of stuff,' he said, stiffly. 'Want to discredit me at Headquarters, eh? The great Detective Lower gets all the credit. Eh! Well, you're wrong. IT WAS ME!'

'All right,' we said, and pulled out our mouth organ.

He was hanged three weeks later.

Turn up the lights.

Lonely Sardine

ELECTROCARDIOGRAM!

Phantasmagoria!

Not that we bear any malice. Simply that we occasionally run short of curses. As Edison once said to the Governor of South Carolina, 'Inspiration is one-tenth perspiration and nine-tenths exasperation.'

We shall therefore talk to you today children, about sardines.

The sardine lives in a tin slum and, due to its environment, there are many feeble-minded sardines in our midst – unaccustomed, mark you, as they are to public speaking.

Environment, said he, throwing his cigarette butt into the waste paper basket in an earnest attempt to burn the office down, is a strange thing. In a very short time, a cat caught in a rat trap becomes distinctly like a dead rat. Given time, the cat may even become deader than the rat. As the poet described the electric chair, 'That burn from which no traveller returns' – that's where it goes.

Speaking of electric chairs, we understand that they are most uncomfortable. A man told us that the accommodation in the electric chair department was shocking. Apart from that, he explained to us that it was one of the few occasions when he didn't have to strap-hang.

They had five goes at him and he blew the fuses out every time.

At the finish, he was so full of electricity that if he pressed his vest button a bell would ring.

Which naturally brings us to the subject of Christmas puddings, of which there are two kinds: the one you put the cheques in and boil it – and ours.

For a large family, we recommend our recipe. All you need is a pound of raisins and a bag of cement. This will last a family of eight for about twelve (12) Christmases. This pudding is hard to beat.

Raisins are very good for you. They contain a lot of iron.

Talk of iron! We knew a man who had so much iron that he was full of nuts and bolts. Matter of fact, he lived on nuts and bolted his meals. After he was operated on for appendicitis he had to be riveted.

If he wanted to turn around, he had to use a spanner. Threw himself under a train and wrecked the train. Rusted away after a long and peaceful life, and was pronounced dead by one of the best engineers in the country.

And if you must have something about sardines, they have no heads, but they carry tales.

Mean to say, they repeat on us. Abysinnia later.

This Gland Cure

While bowling his hoop along George Street, William Hinkler, aged 105, was knocked down by an armoured bus and had his clavicle bashed in. He is now lying in some place. That is to say, some other place. His condition is not serious.

If Bill Voronoff keeps on with his gland treatment, this sort of thing is likely to happen any day. The latest news from Voronoff (by Borronoff and Sir Otto Anaemia) is that by grafting three glands on to the aged frame giant men will live to the age of at least 125 years.

Why in the devil anyone should wish to live in this vale of gas-bills for 125 years surpasses our scientific knowledge.

In plain words which will touch the hearts of the local peasantry, it has us stonkered.

Wanted, boy, about 50 or 60, excellent opportunities for advancement. Apply with parents or guardian.

Thus is the excuse of anti-glandists thrown to the ground and trampled on.

Prolonging life will not cause unemployment. Merely a readjustment. Lovely word, readjustment. We are feeling a bit readjusted ourself.

While peddling eggs to his grandmother, Nicholas Moxon, 132, got his beard caught in the spokes of his tricycle and was thrown to the ground. At Sydney Hospital, Moxon said that he did not blame the tricycle.

Constable Smith, who chased accused in a bath chair, having dropped his gland, has the case in hand.

Developments are expected. Persons having fingerprints are requested to call at Detective office and be arrested.

Gland treatment should be approached carefully. Sneak up on it sideways. Those feeling old are recommended to die now. Don't delay. The price of burial is going up every day. By dying now you save enormous sums of income tax, etc. Especially, etc.

Die now and save.

Bradman and the Burglar

It was 2.30 a. m.
The burglar paused outside the window, jemmy in
hand. A light filtered through the drawn blind, but
it was the dull mumbling from within that held him
hesitant for some minutes.

Then he very gently, very expertly, opened the window. A harsh, stilted voice said, 'Bradman's score now stands at 301.'

Five people were hunched about the loud speaker. Father, mother, two sons, and a daughter. The floor was littered with half-burnt cigarette ends and dead matches. One of the younger men was dotting down Bradman's hits on the back of a player roll which was already half unrolled.

'McCabe cover-drove another for two,' carked the loud speaker.

'Who's bowling?' said the burglar excitedly, stepping into the room.

'Larwood,' said the whole family, without looking up.

'Goodo!' exclaimed the burglar.

Searching the house, he packed up the most portable valuables and was looking for more when a loud, harmonious groan came from around the loud speaker.

'Wot's up!' he cried, rushing in. 'Is 'e out?'

'Clean bowled by that beast Larwood,' sobbed the mother, dabbing her eyes with her handkerchief.

'That's the front door,' said the father. 'Someone answer it.'

No one answered it. 'Tate bowling,' said the announcer.

'I suppose I'll 'ave to go,' grumbled the burglar. A scream came from the room as he opened the door.

'What's wrong here?' said the policeman sternly.

'Richardson's out for one!' murmured the burglar in a hoarse voice.

'My God!' exclaimed the policeman, rushing in.

And at 3.45 a.m., the blear-eyed family dragged itself to bed, the policeman, nervously gazing about for the sergeant, went back to his beat, and the burglar went home, having forgotten his loot.

'Any'ow,' he muttered, as he climbed wearily into his bed. 'I don't care. Five 'undred and sixty-six is goin' to take some catchin'.'

The Last of The Thomases

There was a man named Thomas. There generally is. His surname was Thomas, and his Christian name was Thomas, so his full name was Thomas Thomas.

This is very peculiar.

Thomas's family tree had been ringbarked at his father's death, for Thomas was not married, and he was the last descendant of an honorable family. It looked as if the family could not descend any further. His father died in very romantic circumstances.

He sprained his ankle in Macquarie Street, and a young doctor, seeing him fall, ordered him into hospital and operated on him for appendicitis, so successfully that he died a martyr to science.

On his father's death, Thomas became an orphan, because his mother had died some months before he was born. He graduated as an orphan quite easily.

Thanks to the commonsense laws of this country, all that was necessary for him to become a qualified orphan was that both, or all, of his parents should be dead.

Poor Thomas was cast out into the cruel world to earn his own living. No one can realise the horrors of this unless they have had to earn their own living themselves, so it is no use trying to explain.

It was a bit hot on him, being cast out into the world, though.

With tears in his eyes he watched the landlord kick the door in and seize the furniture his poor old mother had made when she was a girl. Sadly he locked the landlord in, and set fire to the house, and then started out for the cold, hard city.

He had nothing, not even a cat. Not a solitary bell tolled him to come back and be a Lord Mayor.

Going along the road, he struck a kind-hearted motorist, who gave him a lift. Or, rather the motorist struck him. He was lifted about eight feet.

He continued on his way, and at last, after many vicissitudes too numerous to mention, entered the city on his hands and knees.

As he was crawling along in the gutter, a big man in a motor car sliced his ear off with the mudguard, and then, pulling up, greeted him with a hearty laugh.

'I can see by your attitude,' he said, 'that you are looking for work. You look miserable enough to work for practically nothing.

'I might employ you.

'How long is it since you've had a meal?'

'Three weeks,' said Thomas.

That was a lie, as he had only been without food for two weeks. Which just shows you the low cunning of some people.

But the kind gentleman did not suspect that he was

being imposed upon, and he smiled and gently patted Thomas with his foot.

'Hang on to the spare tyre of my car,' he said. 'I will take you with me.'

And so Thomas arrived at the ancestral halls of the kind gentleman, luxuriously hanging on to the spare tyre.

The kind gentleman, who was a retired alderman and very wealthy, allowed him to sleep in the garage, and at first he was bewildered by the luxury which surrounded him, but after a while he got used to it and become more refined.

Thomas progressed rapidly in his master's favour, and after a few months he was doing all the jobs about the place, and the master was able to sack all the servants, including the chauffeur, gardener and the confidential secretary.

Thomas was an ambitious young man, and at 3 a.m., after he had finished his work, he spent the two hours of leisure remaining to him, not in sleep, but in study.

He studied so hard that soon he knew the past form of every horse in the State.

Then the devil tempted him. He embezzled £40 of the kind gentleman's money and went to the races.

The same fate overtook him as has overtook many another who has heeded Satan's promptings.

He won £4000.

Returning to his place of employment, he assaulted the kind gentleman who had befriended him. The kind gentleman never recovered, and although the police were a bit suspicious, they never did anything to Thomas, as a man with £20,000 (it was a three-day race meeting) would never do such a thing. At least that is what the police thought, but then the police are very dense sometimes.

Sir Thomas (for such he was by this time) soon became known far and wide for his good works, and there were more special inquiries held on his doings than any other gentleman in the land. His name became a household word and many people were arrested for saying the word in public.

But Sir Thomas died. Strange to say, he died in an even more romantic way than his father. Driving his car one day, he had been chasing a pedestrian, and at last, tiring of the sport, he ran over him.

The pedestrian had a bottle in his pocket.

The tyre burst, and Sir Thomas was flung out of the car with such force that he spread all over the wall of a nearby building.

When the horrified bystanders scraped him off, he was dead.

So ended the last of the Thomases.

Let this story be a lesson to you, gentle and somewhat dull reader. No matter what people may say, no matter how you are tempted – never be an orphan.

Coming to your house in 2021....

THE LEGENDS OF
LENNIE LOWER

L. Lower, Esky!

Lennie Lower, Australia's greatest humorist of the 1930s, had a wild imagination. Enter here at your own risk!

In **The Legends of Lennie Lower** you will find some of the best of Lower's hair-brained schemes for a perfect home, career or racing win. Here's your chance to unearth The Model Husband, while Turning Out the Aurora Borealis.

With Lower, everything's possible. Allow yourself the childish pleasure of A Grim Fairy Tale; meet Lower's eight grandfathers; Travel the Wilds of Peru. Let Lower do your driving, banking, even your laundry - and live to tell the tale.

Over sixty mad fables set to torment and tease, these are legends from the Master of Mirth. Illustrated by Patrick Cook, with a Backward by Tom Thompson.

ETT IMPRINT, March 2021, 180p, ISBN 978-1-922473-18-9